Osgood and Company

Life of Mme. de la Rochefoucauld

Duchess of Doudeauville, Founder of the Society of Nazareth

Osgood and Company

Life of Mme. de la Rochefoucauld
Duchess of Doudeauville, Founder of the Society of Nazareth

ISBN/EAN: 9783337254773

Printed in Europe, USA, Canada, Australia, Japan

Cover: Foto ©Raphael Reischuk / pixelio.de

More available books at **www.hansebooks.com**

MME. DE LA ROCHEFOUCAULD,

DUCHESS OF DOUDEAUVILLE,

FOUNDER OF THE

SOCIETY OF NAZARETH.

Translated from the French.

BOSTON:

HOUGHTON, OSGOOD AND COMPANY.

The Riverside Press, Cambridge.

1878.

RIVERSIDE, CAMBRIDGE:
STEREOTYPED AND PRINTED BY
H. O. HOUGHTON AND COMPANY.

CONTENTS.

———◆———

LIFE

OF

MADAME DE LA ROCHEFOUCAULD.

---·---

CHAPTER I.

MADEMOISELLE DE MONTMIRAIL.

IT is not without a feeling of respectful
fear that we dare to raise the veil from a
life full of holy mysteries which humility
has always kept carefully hidden. , She,
whom the Lord had prevented with many
graces from her earliest years, concealed
so well everything which might attract
consideration, that her children, her intimate friends, snatched from her only with
difficulty, and as if by surprise, some of
her sublime secrets. If, in order to win
from her one of these desired communica-
tions, you anticipated her by making a con-

fidence, she would answer at times with the same abandonment, betraying herself unconsciously, for from the simplest confession flashed the mild brightness which reveals the precious stone. But one had to be very careful that no expression of admiration escaped him, else would he have saddened a heart which had no inclination but for hidden virtue.

We know then but little of this long existence, which scored by sad trials, shaken by violent storms, yet remained always calm and serene, because it ran on pure and strong, under the eye of God. And even this little that we know we cannot give entire, because, to reveal the heroism of this soul, its patience, its magnanimity, we must discover wrongs done against her of which she never spoke.

Benigne-Augustine-Françoise le Teillier de Louvois de Montmirail was born at Paris the fourth of June, 1764. She was daughter to the Marquis of Montmirail, a man of great merit, and a distinguished pupil of the Fathers of the Company of Jesus. He had married Mademoiselle de Bretonvilliers, then widow of the Marquis of Saint Aulain. The happiness of this second union was of short duration, for after aiding M. de Buffon in the composition of his Natural History, the young marquis, as brilliant knight as learned scholar, went into the army and died there at the moment when he was about to taste, for the second time, the sweetness of paternity. This was a great family grief. All hopes were then turned upon the expected child ; they asked themselves if he would not be heir to the name, and the numerous accessories of his ancestors, and nothing could better paint the natural and most legitimate desires of these great lords, than a speech of the Maréchal d'Estrées : learning that the decisive hour approached, he said to his servants : " If it is a boy, burst open all the doors, and come and tell me; if

it is a girl, let me sleep." Probably they
did not trouble the sleep of the old soldier,
for the marchioness gave birth to a second
daughter, who, after being a friend for her
sister, and the companion of her studies, is
to become later Madame de Montesquiou.

It was thus upon the elder daughter that
the hope of all returned. If, in the midst
of their delusion, the noble parents of this
dear child had caught but a glimpse of her
destiny, they would surely have kneeled
down by the cradle where slept the comforting angel, the support, the preserver of
her family

All that this world holds of most seduc-
tive seemed to combine in an offering to
this delicious little creature : brilliant fortune, a remarkable beauty, a princely position. Nothing that can dazzle was lacking, and there was that to make one tremble, if the elect of earth had not been first
of all a chosen one of heaven. The gifts
of grace, happily, far surpassed those of

nature; the love of God penetrated this child-heart, to illuminate the first rays of intelligence. From the moment that she could fold her hands and lisp the names of Jesus and of Mary, she did it with such grace and sweetness, that one would have said an angel prayed.

They had consecrated her to the blessed Virgin, whose white garments she' wore. When she was three years old, Madame de Mancini, her grandmother, promising herself a fête in giving her the first colored dress, ordered a superb frock, — pink, with silver spangles and fringes. Thinking to delight her, they brought the frock into her room with pomp, to the great admiration of all the women; but the dear child, as if she knew already the bliss of wearing a celestial livery, fixed her great black eyes sadly on the sumptuous apparel, and shed abundant tears when they wished to dress her in it. All the day she begged for her white clothes, and they had to give them back to her.

One day, her maid coming to wake her up, found her radiant in her little bed. "Oh! nurse," she said, "how beautiful it is! Let me see it again; it is heaven and the Holy Virgin! How beautiful. . . . I shall go some day."

There were signs of predestination here. Let us see how God sets about fortifying the souls which He has chosen.

This infancy, so beautiful in its opening, so rich in the gifts of heaven and of earth, ran on sadly, notwithstanding: the father, wise and good, was not there to watch over his girls, and Madame de Montmirail, although animated by excellent intention, could not replace him. Young, beautiful, elegantly clever, haughty, she knew how to preserve a reputation beyond criticism, a thing rare and difficult in her position at the time when she lived. Her original character presented odd contrasts. Noble, generous in her dealings, she was specially charitable towards the poor, to

whom she always gave freely, even after
the emigration, when her fortune was sensibly diminished ; but her private conduct
offered singular minglings, — contradic-
tions, which are explained only by the false
direction given to her youth. In the bosom
of a parliamentary family she had imbibed
Jansenist principles, and withal she surrounded herself with Jesuits. She liked the
great world, pleasure; and in the country
she brought together the people of the
neighborhood — nay, even the peasants, —
and skipped about with them all the evening, as simple and joyous as a child. She
thought, in the light of duty, that the dan-
cing should be over at ten o'clock, but finding it to her taste that it should last until
midnight, she put back the clocks two hours.
This went on for a long time without astonishment being evinced, when people found
the night so far advanced, on getting home.

She had an especial dress for going to
confession, and as at that time they were

particular that the clothing should change with the season, she had to have four toilets entirely set apart for this pious practice.

On the eve of her communions, she fasted and spent the day in profound retreat ; then, in setting forth for mass, she would turn and say to her women : " May God pardon you, young women, as I pardon you." Thinking in this way to have complied with the precept of charity, she approached the holy eucharist with faith.

The marchioness carried the same peculiarity into the management of her children. She took a great deal of trouble about it, but her system of education was severe to harshness. Mademoiselle de Montmirail suffered from it more than her sister. The latter, playful by nature, had the art of disarming her mother by a repartee, thus saving her from the remorse of having been unjust, while little Augustine, timid, fearful, embarrassed, stood speechless through these freaks of temper which she did n't understand. Her tears fell silently, and the marchioness, feeling a reproach for her hasty behaviour, became more irritated than ever.

Exaggerating the best systems of education, she chose to oblige her children to eat everything, and that, without exception, in spite of the protest of temperament ; hence, the younger was shut up a whole day with a plate of carrots, and did n't leave her prison until she had eaten the whole. Mademoiselle Augustine had an unconquerable dislike for onions. She took obediently what her mother had given her, but if her will was submissive, the stomach showed itself rebellious ; then pitilessly they forced the poor child to take back the rejected food. There was this other thing that tortured her, — when her mother, raising her voice, would say to her suddenly :

" Speak, mademoiselle, say something at once."

At this unseasonable order, the dear little girl troubled, struck dumb, was bereft of voice and words. A second injunction finished the confusion of her ideas ; tears got the better of her, and for her consolation the marchioness would add : —

" Kneel down, miss, and stay in the middle of the room until you have spoken."

The child would bend her little head to show herself docile, but it was often without result ; and she related, later in life, that one day, after trying her best, she had been very pleased to be able to say, " There are three cracks in the ceiling." She was far from being deficient in intelligence, as we shall see, in following this pious life.

She was greatly loved by those who surrounded her ; her uncles, her sisters, her governesses, the maids, all showed her affection, and consoled her a little for the severity of her mother. The Marshal d'Estrées called her Bellotte ; this truly remarkable beauty might have become disastrous to her, for she heard it incessantly praised ; but at the age of six she was looking at herself in the glass with satisfaction, when, instead of her own charming face, she saw only a death's head. Was this the effect of an excited imagination, or one of the mercies which God sometimes grants to favoured souls? We should not dare to say ; but it is certain that at the age of seventy or eighty years, the Duchess of Doudeauville still spoke with tears of the impression produced by this image of death. From this moment, the fear of offending God made her look upon beauty as a sad advantage and a real danger ; this thought never abandoned her, even in the midst of the most brilliant successes.

Every morning the governess led the two little girls into the marchioness' room, whilst she made her toilet. After kissing their mother's hand, they would learn their lessons by her side, and were severely punished when they did n't know them very well.

Mademoiselle Augustine was only seven years old when she lost her great-uncle, the Marshal d'Estrées, who loved her dearly. The brave soldier died like a Christian hero; when they brought him the sacraments, in spite of keen suffering, he tried to rise to receive our Lord. During this time his little niece was praying with fervour in the adjoining room; she already understood that something very solemn was taking place; that she was losing a protector, but already, too, she thought of eternity.

Every year, under the charge of their governess, the two children made a six months' stay, or so, on an estate called Binanville, near Mantes. Madame Montmirail often went to see them, but her appearance was always the signal for some punishment, and yet Mademoiselle Augustine applied herself earnestly to her studies; her great happiness was to hear mass which a venerable Franciscan often came to say in the chapel of the castle. He had noticed the angelic child, and, touched by her piety, he often interposed as mediator between her and her mother. Her dolls, the walks in a nice little wood, sweet cakes, the milk which they drank at Jeanette's mother's farm, — all these held a good place in her childish recollections. They were the little girls' greatest amusements. Thanks to their affection, Jeanette was well educated, afterwards well settled, and they went to see her with great pleasure.

As soon as their age allowed a more continuous application, Madame Montmirail chose the best professors for her daughters, adding accomplishments to their graver studies. Madame Leprince de Beaumont, who has composed excellent works for the young, gave them lessons for three years; she became much attached to her two pupils, and when she left them to go to Spain, she wrote very affectionately to Mademoiselle Augustine, who was pleased and

2

proud. A disciple of Rollin replaced this
excellent governess as professor of history, and interested the children, whose
taste was beginning to be formed ; he was
a pious man ; he interspersed his lessons
with sage reflections, which suited the serious character of Mademoiselle Augustine ;
he spoke often of her father, this father
whom she had never known, and whom
everybody knew and admired. Each and
all seemed to say that if he had lived, he
would have made her happy. Did these
praises call out deep regrets and compari-
sons which we can easily understand ? We
do not know. The dear child never complained, and never accused anybody. Long
after, when, in looking back to her early
years, people reminded her of what she
must have suffered, she answered simply :
" My mother was virtuous ; and if it is true
that she was sharp and severe toward me,
I thank God for it as a great boon ; for, if
from my childhood I had found a friend in

her, with my sensitive and ardent nature I should have attached myself strongly to the creature."

It was, then, to keep this young heart quite for Himself, to prepare it for great struggles, that our Lord initiated it in suffering on the threshold of life, revealing to it the secrets of His love.

One day Madame de Montmirail sends for her elder daughter, and says in a tone which admits of no reply : —

"You have told a falsehood, miss, and, in consequence, you are to leave my roof instantly."

Little Augustine, who had only answered some foolish question simply and timidly, climbs, all dazed, into a carriage, and presently reaches the convent door, where they introduce her as a little culprit. The nuns of the Visitation, greatly astonished, were not long in finding in their new pupil a good, sweet, and pious child, who soon won their affection. At first, she mourned sadly her sister, her nurse, her belongings ; but, little by little, the atmosphere of gentleness, of silence, of love of God, which she breathed in this religious house dissipated her grief, and the pious asylum became for her a place of delights, whose peace and sweetness were grateful to her soul. She learned there the charm of friendship, for despite the contrast of their characters, she formed a close intimacy with Mademoiselle de Sinetti. United in their studies and their games, the school-girls were later bound to one another by the same maternal griefs, and up to a very old age, the virtuous Duchess of Doudeauville sustained and encouraged the brilliant Duchess of Caderousse, who always felt for her friend a tenderness mingled with reverence.

This sojourn at the Visitation, ten months long only, was marked by a great event, — a memorable date whose anniversary Madame de Doudeauville kept all her life with renewed joy and gratitude. The years, instead of weakening this feeling, served, on the contrary, only to increase it ; for, towards the end of her life, when her soul seemed to begin to be indifferent to the things of earth, while alive only to heavenly things, it was enough to speak the name of Saint John in her presence, to irradiate her face and make her start with joy : " Oh ! " she would say, " that is the day of my first communion ! "

What took place in the heart of the twelve years' child at this solemn moment ? Doubtless God made her to taste marvellously His holy presence ; for after a long thanksgiving, when all the companions about her had disappeared, Mademoiselle de Montmirail, on her knees, saw nothing, heard nothing ; she seemed transported to heaven. The nun detailed to call her, not daring to disturb her meditation, stopped, filled with respect, before this child lost in the presence of God. But as the prayers still went on, fearing for her health, they decided to interrupt her. "What! already!" she said sadly, and it cost her a great effort to leave her prie-Dieu.

After her communion, she felt herself strongly impelled by the desire to consecrate herself entirely to her Lord. The life of the convent was full of attraction for her recollected soul. This calm, this regular life, suited her character much better than the agitation of the age. The kindness of her teachers, the friendship of her companions, expanded her heart, so that she experienced a great sadness when her mother, on the very evening of this great day, announced to her that she was to return immediately to her house at Louvois. She ventured timidly to make a request. "Until now," she said, "I have thought of nothing but my first communion; if you would allow me to spend three or four days more here, to prepare myself for going back to the world, I should be most grateful."

Madame de Montmirail willingly yielded to her daughter's wish, who continued her retreat with a fervour and seriousness far beyond her years. Let us listen to her own impressions, revealed in a moment of effusion.

" All that the world esteemed seemed to me despicable, and I could n't understand how one could attach himself to these things. From the gallery where I was fervently praying, I could see the nuns prostrate themselves, with their faces against the ground, spending long hours before the tabernacle. I thought them happy beyond all expression, and in my childishness, I kissed the walls of the cloister, where I would fain have stayed always. I loved dearly Saint François de Sales, whom I called our holy founder ; my desire to enrol myself among his daughters became so pressing, that one day, after my meditation, without understanding to what I was going to engage myself, seeing only the happiness of belonging entirely to God, I had on my lips the perpetual vow of virginity, when I thought I heard distinctly these words: 'No — in the world, against all thine inclination.' Then, trembling, and bursting into tears, I answered: 'As Thou wouldst have it, Lord, but let the will of my mother be the expression of Thine.' And it seemed to me as if I were to practice the virtues of the cloister, without tasting its sweets, to apply myself to humility in the midst of grandeur, to poverty in the lap of riches, to mortification under the outward appearance of well-being, to the purest modesty amid the vanities and follies of the century. This sacrifice cost me a great deal; but I could not be mistaken about the will of God, and I prayed to Him to aid me in conquering my repugnance."

The three days of grace having elapsed, Mademoiselle Augustine, perfectly resigned, fell back under the severe and fanciful yoke of her mother, who continued to punish her for the merest trifles ; the most frequent offences came from some slight omission of etiquette, from an awkwardness caused by timidity — the exceeding fear of that pitiless look, which paralyzed the young girl, just as it had embarrassed the child. For instance, eight days after her marriage, she was condemned by her mother to dine alone at a table of penitence, in a corner of the dining-room, because she had made her courtesy badly, in entering the drawing-room.

The torture of these sad days began in the early morning, for the coiffure of this period demanded a great deal of time, and the maid took two hours every day for arranging a superb head of hair, which Mademoiselle de Montmirail would gladly have committed to the scissors. An extreme sensitiveness made of these two hours a veritable martyrdom. She spent them in complete immobility, while thinking of the crown of thorns.

Meanwhile, everybody was absorbed by the marriage-plans for this beautiful and rich heiress. She alone never thought of them. Of suitors there could be no lack for one who joined to her personal charms every social advantage ; among them figured a Spanish grandee of the first class, placed over the Duchy of Doudeauville in the Boulonnais. People asked each other who would be the favoured mortal chosen for such an alliance. In the young ladies' room great names were mentioned, the most brilliant cavaliers were passed in review. All at once the Viscount of Rochefoucauld was presented to Mademoiselle de Montmirail, with whom, until then, he had had nothing to do. Great excitement among the people of the house. What is he about ? They make inquiry. He has an only son, but he is still a child. Is it for the sake of some nephew ? They are all pretty indifferent matches.

It is really, then, for the son who is travelling; they are astonished not to see him return; people get lost in surmises, to which Miss Augustine is a complete stranger.

The Viscount of Rochefoucauld-Surgères represented one of the younger branches of that illustrious family, which, originally from the province of Guienne, is connected with the dukes of Aquitaine under the Carlovingians and with the lords of Lusignan in the time of the Crusades, when the family inaugurated its coat of arms.

The branch of the Montendre-Surgères begins in the sixteenth century, in the person of Louis de la Rochefoucauld, fifth son of Duke François, who had the honour of holding over the baptismal font, King François I., and of giving him his name.

One day, Mademoiselle de Montmirail's maid, after taking more than usual pains with the hair-dressing, presents her with an extraordinarily elegant dress. Surprised, she asks what this means.

" But, does n't Mademoiselle know that the Viscount of Rochefoucauld is to come to-day, to ask her in marriage ? "

Without answering, the young girl hurries the finishing of her toilet, and runs and throws herself into her mother's lap.

" You know," she cried, " that I am unhappily destined to have a great fortune. I would like never to leave you, and if I should have the unhappiness to survive you, I would consecrate all my fortune to doing good works."

" Impossible ! " replied the marchioness, with icy coldness, " the Viscount of Rochefoucauld is to ask you for his son ; he will bring him this evening ; examine him carefully ; and if he does n't suit you, you will tell me, and I will find some one else for you."

" I have no investigations to make, mother," rejoined Mademoiselle de Montmirail, " and if I must marry, I accept the one whom you have chosen."

"Very well," said the marchioness, with the same indifference, apparently without noticing her daughter's emotion.

She retired with a very full heart, but decided upon the sacrifice.

In the evening the reception was magnificent ; but imagine the general effect ! Mademoiselle de Montmirail, dazzling in her grace and freshness, found herself opposite to a little boy not fourteen years old, thin, puny, delicate, with childish features, utterly embarrassed, and still more bored with the part he was made to play. On learning that his marriage was at stake, he exclaimed sadly, "Alas ! I shan't be able to amuse myself any more."

The two heroes of the evening scarcely looked at each other ; and when Madame de Montmirail asked her daughter if young Ambroise suited her, "As well as anybody else," she answered.

There were several other solemn interviews, when the future pair exchanged not a word. What must this young girl have felt — so serious, of a judgment beyond her years — when she sought in this poor little fellow — timid, shame-faced, disconcerted at the premature part he was playing — a counsellor, a support, the centre of all her affections. But if she suffered, her height and her beauty greatly alarmed poor Ambroise, who hardly dared to look at her, and asked himself if he was doomed to spend his life in an uncomfortable constraint.

No dream of happiness, we see, presided over this strange alliance. In putting her seal to the most important act of her life, the young girl submits to an order which, she thinks, comes directly from heaven ; she hears in her ears the sound of the words which destroyed her dearest hopes, — "In the world, against all thine inclination." She accepts, but with the resignation of a generous victim. As for the child of fourteen years, who tremblingly signs a solemn contract, he executes with timidity the will of his father, as he would have performed a penance.

On the 10th of April, 1779, were seen through the open folding-doors of the Hotel de Louvois, the Swiss guardsmen, in full uniform, magnificent carriages, horses richly caparisoned, liveried servants bearing bouquets of flowers, assembled in the courtyard, — all the stir of a magnificent fête. Soon, in the midst of a brilliant cortége, appeared a lovely and majestic young girl, whose emotion was so keen that all the delicate orange blossoms trimming her dress seemed agitated by a breath of the morning air. One looked in vain for the hero of the fête, amid the great lords, and was resigned, perforce, to find him in a little boy, who, in spite of all his efforts to hold up his head, hardly reached the shoulder of his fiancée. The poor child paid dearly that day for all the honours of the moment, and his future happiness. As if to throw out better the smallness of his stature, all the Swiss Guards were men of six feet and more; so that everybody smiled who saw him, and the contrast which he made to his charming companion drew the attention more upon him than upon her, — a preference with which he could very easily have dispensed.

They laughed, then, and we should perhaps have had a feeling of sadness, or at least of astonishment at this singular assemblage. And yet, time has proved that if appearances were deceptive, as is so often the case, this time, at least, the reality was much better than the promise. This child will grow truly worthy in all points, — in fortune, name, and in the high offices which he is called upon to discharge. Upright, good, loyal, refined, generous, he will make the happiness of his virtuous wife, so far as it is possible for a creature to satisfy a heart which aspires to the divine union only.

Did not the illustrious patron saints of Augustine and Ambroise agree to form a holy alliance and to bless it from the height of heaven?

We may believe it when we see the treasures that this brave woman heaped up for eternity, and the good which she did in her new family.

If even then she had been able to read the heart of the timid youth who accompanied her to the altar, she would have admired his having kept the integrity of his faith in the midst of a thousand errors and prejudices.

Fearing that they might lose him as they had his two older brothers, his parents had sent him to the country a few days after his birth, where he stayed until he was six years old, running wild about the fields, in snow, ice, and mud, breathing the pure air, and revelling in perfect liberty. Their wish was to strengthen his health, but Providence, to save and preserve his

3

soul, had placed at his side an excellent nurse, an honest and simple peasant, who, in giving him her material care, sowed in his soul the seeds of truth. She read his catechism to him, to which little Ambroise listened with great attention. His lively imagination was kindled by the lives of the saints, and his natural bravery prompted him to long for martyrdom. The pious nurse, alarmed at the skeptical atmosphere breathed by this child, the object of her tenderness, and desirous to preserve his faith, made him kneel down every morning with his face turned towards the village church ; then, showing him the steeple, she would say : —

"Look at that cross ; our Lord is there. He can grant us all that we ask of Him. Let us pray together, and say with me : My God, grant that false doctrines may never corrupt my heart."

This prayer was so deeply engraved on the dear child's memory, that many years after, when a skeptical teacher, filled with the false ideas of the day, intended to instil the poison of incredulity into the soul of the young man, under an attractive form, feeling an instinctive fear, he opened the door of his alcove, before taking his lesson, and kneeling down behind the curtain, repeated with faith, — " My God, grant that false doctrines may never corrupt my heart." Thanks to this simple prayer he escaped many and great dangers.

But no interchange of words had made known to the young woman the disposition of her new mentor ; she entered into the unknown, relying only upon the Divine will, which she had sought to know, and from which, after the example of the Saviour, she derived all her support.

Cardinal de la Rochefoucauld performed the marriage ceremony. After a sumptuous wedding-feast, and a magnificent party, young Ambroise, now Duke de Doudeauville, glad to see the day end in which his only pleasure had been to hear the drum beat, went immediately to Versailles with his tutor. As to the bride of fifteen years, she was intrusted to the care of her step-mother, the Viscountess de la Rochefoucauld, and continued with her during her life of young girlhood. This protecting influence, though quite different from that of Madame de Montmirail, was even less reasonable, as we shall soon find.

CHAPTER II.

THE CHRISTIAN IN THE WORLD.

A NEW life in a new world opens before the young and charming woman, who, to her great regret, occupies the thoughts of a brilliant and idle public. She has passed, by direct transition, from the table of penance to the sumptuous spectacles of court festivals. If she is sometimes intimidated by all this, if the pomp offends her modesty, she is never dazzled by it, and in following her over what is called the theatre of her success, we shall follow her happily, always through an arena of pious combats, assisting towards the triumph of her virtue.

The Viscountess de la Rochefoucauld, proud of her daughter-in-law, insisted that she should wear rich and elegant costumes

to receive her wedding visits. Society at
that time was all infatuation ; people were
carried away by the idol of the day ; the
flame burned bright and fast, but generally
was very fleeting. The beauty of the young
duchess became the object of general admiration ; it was the common talk ; it was
only, who could see her ; people crowded
into the drawing-rooms where she was to
appear, and when, at last, she was announced, the hostess in a loud voice would
order the chandelier and all the candles to
be lighted. Shamed by such display, she
would inwardly pray God to save her from
these dangerous honours.

In this high position, the then custom
demanded that a bride should be presented
to the public accompanied by all the wedding train ; she must go to the opera, and
there, surrounded by her relatives, make a
low courtesy to the parterre and to the
boxes, which answered by applause. The
cheers called forth by the young duchess

were so enthusiastic, so redoubled, that after the necessary acknowledgments, she retired to the back of her box as soon as possible.

When Madame de la Rochefoucauld presented her at court, the great gallery at Versailles was filled with curious courtiers; they climbed up on chairs to see her the better, and the murmurs· of admiration which reached her ears increased her embarrassment and emotion to such a degree, that after receiving a thousand tokens of kindness from the king, the princes and princesses, she was obliged to ask permission of the queen not to go to the play in the evening. Several attacks of fever expiated this fragile triumph.

A grand quadrille was announced at court; the duchess was begged to take part in it; and an invitation was a polite order which one could not resist. Putting aside, then, her fears and her repugnance, she went to the many rehearsals indispensable to the perfect execution of an entertainment which absorbed all the elegant world. We can understand what must have been the license of that frivolous youth, distracted with pleasure and success, during the *laisser-aller* common to rehearsals of this kind. Madame de Doudeauville learned only to dance. Her grave modesty held the boldest at a distance, and she compelled this volatile society to admire her ingenuousness and her virtue.

It was at Versailles, first of all, that this famous quadrille was to take place. All the assemblage of ladies, jealous of her who eclipsed them without taking any trouble about it, made a plot to get their hair dressed before her, and to keep the celebrated Léonard up to the last moment. During this small feminine intrigue one of the coterie slips out and goes in search of the young duchess to enjoy her agitation and bad temper. But what is her astonishment when she finds her tranquilly seated, and in the pious occupation of repeating vespers, for it was a Sunday. She returns without delay, edified and disconcerted at the same time. Soon after Léonard arrives quite out of breath, and exclaims, " Ah! the naughty things ! they have left me only five minutes. Well, for all that, your hair shall be well dressed, and better than theirs." And so it was.

This victory mattered little to the humble duchess, but she was pleased with the good man's kind intention, and gave him a token of her gratitude.

The success of the evening was complete ; and while the Viscountess de la Rochefoucauld was intoxicated by the homage lavished on her daughter-in-law, she herself said with pious fright, —

" Oh, mother, mother ! Do you wish then to ruin me ? "

Whatever excited so much admiration alarmed her delicate conscience. She looked upon it as an occasion of sin. And this involuntary connivance with the devil horrified her. Once, only once, having heard some one say : " Her eyes are beautiful, especially when she raises them to heaven," by an instinctive movement she looked up at the cornice ; but instantly, seized with remorse and confusion, she dropped her eyelids and reproached herself her life long for having been surprised into vanity.

It was she who was chosen to beg in the chapel at Versailles, on the reception of the knights of the order. She acquitted herself so well, that only a short time after, contrary to the court usage, she was invited to beg a second time. This innovation was due to the presence of Paul I., on whom the king wished the French ladies to make a good impression. The queen dispatched a messenger with all speed to find the Duchess of Doudeauville, then at Turny, to persuade her to come back to court, and she lent her own diamonds for the occasion.

This was the outer life of this young woman from her fifteenth to her seventeenth year. We know her tastes, her inclination to piéty. Let us see, if, in the family life at least, she can be compensated and give free vent to the impulse of her faith.

The Hotel la Rochefoucauld Surgères was at this period the rendezvous of the philosophers and wits of the day. All the fashionable theories were discussed there, — singular, or rather monstrous combination of distorted gospel truths and human passions. Philanthropy, indifference in religious matters, took the place of the strong and true virtues which Christianity alone can produce. Pure faith, sacred dogma were left to the simple, the ignorant, to women and children. The intelligent, the strong-minded, must content themselves with a religion, vague, ideal, indefinite. All the Rochefoucauld family were imbued with these false doctrines, young Ambroise alone excepted ; and we understand what she must have suffered, who came to this society adorned even more richly with virtue than with beauty. Her attitude, though always gentle, seemed austere to this jesting company, witty and pleasure-loving. Her faith was attacked in pleasantry and sarcasm ; without daring to address themselves directly to her, they threw ridicule upon her dearest beliefs. At first she was sadly astonished ; her soul had not suspected that there could be so much impiety in the world. To amazement succeeded painful sufferings. This laughing, these strange words, caused her intense agony. They seemed to ask her with a mocking look, Where is thy God ? What torture for a soul so pure, so consumed with zeal for the Lord's house.

Still she was silent, for though these blasphemies changed in no wise the purity of her faith, she would not have been able to defend it outwardly ; the studies of that

time were not deep enough to enable her
to combat the numerous arguments with'
which she was plied. She felt their false-
ness, but she had sought in religion the
light for the fulfilling of her duties, and not
the refutation of doubts which had never
ruffled her mind. Her silence was set
down as stupidity. She felt this judgment,
and suffered from it, but she appeared not
to notice it.

Before her marriage, she had requested
freedom in the exercise of her religion;
they had promised it to her, and, notwithstanding, all the days of abstinence became
days of torment to her. Alone she fasted
at the table of her father-in-law, and each
time there was a fresh scene. In vain, her
mother-in-law, who was very fond of her,
attempted to interpose between her and the
Viscount of Rochefoucauld; he promised
to hold his tongue, but immediately began
again. His voice was by turns ironical and
impatient, and the mortifying words were

accompanied by sarcasms which pierced the heart of the young Christian. She dreaded this time of trial to such an extent that a part of the night between Thursday and Friday was often passed by her in prayer. Bursting into tears at the foot of her crucifix, she would ask for courage to bear the struggle, and when the hour came, she commended herself again to God, and could hardly control the beating of her heart when she sat down to table. When there, she seemed a marble statue, hearing and understanding nothing.

On entering her new family, she had got permission to go to mass every day, but it was not long before this one consolation was refused her, on the pretext that it tired the horses. She did not insist, wishing to reserve the right of exacting that she should be taken at least on the Sundays, and days of obligation. This prudent and firm attitude commanded respect, and she had the happiness, amid so many difficulties, never to fail in keeping a precept of the church.

Looking upon a frequenting of the theatre as dangerous, she did not wish to go, and privately implored her mother-in-law to come to her aid. Madame de la Rochefoucauld, wishing to please her new daughter, had recourse to a hundred subterfuges to postpone the theatre evenings, which came three times a week. Sometimes she would complain of headache, she did not feel well just as they were about to set out, or perhaps she did n't care about the piece they were to play. In spite of these maternal devices, it was necessary to go now and then, when the young duchess, preoccupied with the thought that she might be offending God, would follow the large crowd with indifference. In order not to participate voluntarily in the acting, she tried to find some distraction, and in consequence, passed for a person of very little clever-

ness. Her coldness contrasted strongly
with the enthusiasm of her surrounding.
This same coldness while listening to a
romance was revolting. They began to
question her sensibility, which was most
painful to her. " She appreciates nothing, she understands nothing," they said.
These words were accompanied by signifi-
cant winks and smiles of pity. The conversation would stop when she came into
the room, or else it would go on, as if they
did n't know that she had appeared; all
this performance did not escape her, and
she had to use great self-control to seem
insensible to it.

She was far from being indifferent, however; all noble and elevated sentiments
found an echo in her, and all good works
sympathy.

If she shut her ears to all reading which
attacks morals and religion, she was interested almost too keenly in what are
called good novels. During the two first

years which followed on her marriage, it often happened that she was taken well into the night by the charm of a story. Once, in the midst of a thrilling passage, she heard the clock strike four in the morning. There was a moral awaking. Surprised at this fascination, she stops, reflects a moment, — "If this reading is not bad, it is at least a great waste of time," and therewith she shuts the book never to open it again, or any other of the same kind. From that moment she always gave to her intellect and her heart the simple and solid food of truth. She might often be seen before the tabernacle with a little book which made her joy, and which she put in the number of her dearest treasures. Relying on the old friendship at the Jesuit College, which had united her father, the Marquis de Montmirail, and Alphonse de Liguori, she had written to this zealous apostle of the religion of Mary and of the Blessed Sacrament, to ask his prayers and

4

blessing.   The answer, accompanied by a copy of " Visits to the Blessed Sacrament," was received with joyful gratitude.

Whilst the young woman bore with patience and firmness secret and incessant little persecutions, the Duke of Doudeauville, at a great distance, had the same struggle to sustain, and opposed a passive resistance.   We find his own testimony in his memoirs.

" The persons to whom I owed my respect and confidence, had been giving me for a year or two books on materialism, and the worst works of Voltaire, in order to shape my mind and educate my heart ; moreover, there were conversations in the same spirit which were to explain my readings, and give force to them ; but it was not successful, and I made no progress in this kind of study.

" To escape these singular conversations, and these readings, which I understood very well, I gave myself the appearance of not hearing, and preferred to pass for a poor fool rather than to deserve the title of strong-minded, so much coveted by the young nobility of the time.

" As soon as I could, I would run to my room, fall on my knees and pray God not to let the religion be stifled and annihilated which He alone had put into my soul. It gave me content, submission, happiness, each time that I discharged my· Christian obligations, just as it has since given me consolation, strength, resignation, and love of my duties."

The Duke of Doudeauville adds that he returned from time to time to see his young wife, but as they were never left alone, they could not freely exchange any expression of sentiments. They tried to make this good by their correspondence, which grew tender, active, interesting, both finding great pleasure in this commerce of thoughts ; but all at once, through some inexplicable whim, the Rochefoucauld family took alarm at the frequent letters : What could these children be talking about, who did n't know each other? Was the young duchess, perhaps, using too strong a Christian influence? To convince themselves, they opened her writing-desk during her absence, and carried off, to her great regret, the very innocent subject of her favorite recreation.

And yet her new family desired to make her happy. If they interfered with her tastes, it was to give her more enjoyments ; if they attacked her faith, her pious practices, it was to free her from false prejudices, from a servile bondage ; to raise her to the level of her century. The Viscount of Rochefoucauld particularly, took upon himself to make over this education, which he found out of date. He saw very soon that he must give up the scheme, but if he must needs resign himself to see by his fireside a mediæval figure, which flattered his self-love in every other respect, at all events he

was very sure that no member of the house·
hold shared such retrograde notions. Now,
quite contrary to the impression of the
skeptical philosopher, the influence of the
brave woman was beginning to be felt.
How could one resist this vigorous sweetness, this patient firmness joined to a goodness so true and so touching! There was so
much delicacy in her demeanour, so great
nobleness in her sentiments, elevation in
her thoughts, all relations with her were so
easy, so pleasant, that they had to submit
to evidence and recognize that the heart of
the fervent Christian contained treasures of
tenderness, of devotion and fidelity. The
viscountess was the first to yield to this
mastery of virtue. She loved her daughter-
in-law even more than her own children.
Madame de Durtal, eldest sister to the
Duke de Doudeauville, also felt for her a
fond and deep affection. She was a charming person, full of wit and talent, but these
natural qualities lacked the solid basis of

faith and the perfume of piety. We shall see, later, how she felt herself drawn to God by the power of good example.

But it was only little by little that Madame de Doudeauville exercised this gentle sway. Before gaining the souls so dear to her, her own had much to suffer, and her isolation was still very complete, when they announced to her that her husband would soon arrive.

This tidings filled her with hope. She had such a need of affection, of a legitimate affection, good, simple, true, constant . . . . was she about to experience it ? . . . .

She fell to dreaming of happiness as her heart understood it: the conformity of views and sentiments, reciprocal esteem, the *union* in doing good, the sharing of joys and sorrows; she had much to give : what would she receive in return ? The letters of the young man led her to hope that he had kept himself upright and pious ; but he had had such bad surroundings ! That last

journey to Italy with his father, might it
not have changed his ideas? All these
thoughts chased each other through the
head of the young duchess, and preoccupied her; she prayed much, and compelled
herself to appear gay.

The day being come; when the noise of
wheels is heard in the court-yard they all
rush to greet the travellers; the young
woman, agitated, well-nigh frightened, fol-
lows the move. The carriage stops, the
carriage door opens, but the poor husband,
under the pressure of an emotion which
confuses his wits, looks without seeing anything, and stands motionless . . . . An expressive sign from his father wakes him up.
He gets down, opens his arms to the first
person he meets, and pressing him tenderly
to his heart, he exclaims : " My dear wife,
what happiness to see you again!" It was
an old steward of sixty years who received
his fond embrace . . . . A few steps off,
the duchess, pale, astonished at the slight,

looks upon the scene, of which she was never able to speak with indifference, even in her old age. But how can we paint her despair when she sees her husband, recovering from the mistake, place himself before her, and declaim in an emphatic tone, with ridiculous gestures, a bit of poetry of questionable taste. "Oh me!" she says inwardly, "he will be worse than his father!" And this thought, the saddest that ever crossed her soul, caused her to faint. They had great difficulty in bringing her to herself again.

Being taken to her room, she received the most zealous care, especially from her father-in-law, the author of all this comedy, who was in despair at the serious result. Wishing to convince himself of the intelligent capacity of his daughter-in-law, he had amused himself by making these bad verses, and had arranged the programme for his son, too obedient on this occasion. "If she accepts these compliments," he said to himself, " she is a fool of the first order." The ordeal was terrible, but she was happy in its consequences. Monsieur de la Rochefoucauld began to suspect that there was as much intelligence as virtue in this young woman, about whom the judgment had been so much mistaken ; it was necessary that the young man should make amends for the nonsense of his father ; and thus the young couple had a good and frank explanation, which did more to link their lives than the best endeavours of months would have done. Making the most of their liberty, the two had a few years of happiness as complete as this world can offer.

This sweet intimacy was momentarily interrupted by the obligation to appear at the court festivities, so brilliant during the first years of the reign of Louis XVI. The Tuileries, Versailles, Trianon, Marly, each in turn kindled with the festive fire. Hunting-parties, balls, dramatic parties, concerts, amusements of all kinds, succeeded each other.

Alas, it was not long before the thorns hidden beneath these flowers began to be cruelly felt, and already slander and calumny mingled their voices with peals of laughter in this volatile society which was playing on a precipice. The Duchess of Doudeauville, well received by the queen, the princesses, and especially by Madame Elizabeth, moved amid these gayeties with grace and dignity. It was easy to see that whether she won approbation or not, it was all one to her. The charm which emanated from her silenced the expressions of contempt for the great youth of her husband and his excessive timidity.

Thus the duke relates that, happening to be one day at Marly, the king invited him to sup with his family. Hardly was he seated at table, when he felt himself attacked by sleep so heavily, that, despite all his efforts, he fell into a somnolent condition, without speaking or moving, which lasted from the beginning of the repast to the end. The duchess, unable to rouse him from his lethargy, busied herself so well to divert attention from him, that Louis XVI., who was perfectly cognizant of this grave impropriety, made as though he had not noticed it.

A little while after, the Duke of Doudeauville, wide-awake this time, had an opportunity, in his turn, to take his wife's part. The way in which he acquitted himself reflects credit on the two.

Dining at the house of the Prince de Condé, he had the pleasure to be seated next one of those presumptuous young persons who have a way of speaking and touching upon every subject in an arbitrary fashion, and who insist above all upon distinguishing themselves by a spirit of opposition. Among a hundred different chance remarks, this young man, without suspecting that he was addressing her hus-

band, pronounces the name of the Duchess
de Doudeauville. No interruption. . . . .
He goes on: "She is a woman whose
charms are universally praised, but she
has n't enough talent to please me." And
the young pedant states reasons, which,
without calling out any words of surprise,
make his silent auditors smile. All at once
one of the guests accosts the Duke of
Doudeauville by name. His poor neighbor red, confused, embarrassed, stammers,
attempts to retract his first assertion.
"Calm yourself, my dear friend," said the
duke, "be calm, I beg. For a woman like
Madame de Doudeauville, the essential
thing is that she should please her husband. Console yourself, then; your opinion will not change mine. I find my wife
accomplished in every particular."

In proportion as we advance in this narrative, which we do not fear to call the life
of a saint, we shall always find new proofs

that faith, intelligent religion, illumined piety, are admirably united in her heart with the tender and legitimate affections which they sanctify in order that they may be eternal.

Madame de Doudeauville loved very dearly her sister, the Countess of Montesquiou. Brought up by a peculiar mother, they had comforted each other in their childish sorrows. And when married, they continued to see one another as often as possible. Their esteem and support in the practice of duty amid numerous difficulties was mutual. No cloud ever passed across their friendship.

After the death of the Marquis of Courtenvaux, their grandfather, when the will was read to the two young women, Madame de Montesquiou being thereby advantaged as much as possible, — Madame de Doudeauville thus dispossessed of a part of her rights, threw herself into her sister's arms, crying: "How glad I am!" She rejoiced to see an equilibrium of fortunes somewhat restored in this way.

This death of the marquis in July of the year 1781, called the duchess to the succession of the estates of Montmirail, whose title her father had inherited, without the enjoyment of possession. When she went to claim the estate, there were great fêtes throughout the country. She bore her honours with charming grace, and everywhere showed her kindness and generosity towards the poor — in very truth, such a châtelaine as the most brilliant poet's imagination could paint.

Faithful to the old traditions of honour and chivalry, the Duke of Doudeauville had gone into the army, and was obliged to leave his family often for a longer or shorter time. He suffered from this separation, and profited by all his free moments to return to a wife whom he esteemed and cherished more and more each day, whose example and counsels he

felt necessary to counterbalance the per-
fidious insinuations of dangerous friends.
Invulnerable, as far as his principles were
concerned, he was on the point of giving
up religious practices, because of yielding
to feelings of exaggerated scrupulousness,
which had the more influence over him,
as his natural caution predisposed him to
anxiety. His position obliged him to take
part in the court fêtes and amusements.
People were astonished to see him approach the sacraments in the midst of such
a worldly atmosphere; it was a want of
respect for holy things. . . . . These reflections made an impression upon him,
and he was going so far as to deprive himself of his paschal communion, when a free
and confidential talk with his wife showed
him the snare. She succeeded admirably
in defining the difference between a duty
of position and a simple natural temptation.

She who watched over the soul of her

husband in this way had another mission to fulfil : the wise and faithful wife was to become in a still more perfect degree the model mother.

CHAPTER III.

AMONG the pictures which filial piety preserves with religious respect, because they recall the traits of a saint and of a mother, there is one which has our preference, and which our eyes consider with delight. It is not just yet that of the venerated grandmother, but it is a much finer picture than the beauty before which the crowd paused in admiration ; it is the young mother, beaming with happiness, who carries in her arms her precious treasure. Joy, love, tenderness, give a new colouring to the habitual expression of angelic sweetness, and the picture is perfect, for little Ernestine is like a bud close to the flower. Happy in existence, she rests smilingly on her mother's bosom.

5

Happy, indeed, the child placed under such an ægis! . . . . It has all the blessings of earth, and all the favours of heaven. She who clasps it with ecstasy in her arms, who watches by its cradle, is not only careful to ward off any danger which threatens this frail existence, but she seeks for the divine breath in the little creature which the Lord has given into her keeping, and then respect mingles with her tenderness. To preserve innocence, to keep this little heart from the attacks of evil, to fill it with love and faith,— this was the habitual thought, the constant preoccupation of the Duchess of Doudeauville. She knew that very early impressions, even before a reasonable age, are keen and lasting, and therefore was very careful that her daughter, and the son whom she had two years after, should have only good examples before their eyes. Obliged to have somebody to take her place at times with the children, she chose with the greatest care the individuals who were to help her in developing these young intelligences, and in feeding them with truth. No ridiculous stories, no absurd tales ; and yet the lively and ardent imagination of Ernestine and Sosthènes had a share in the marvellous which charms from the very cradle, for the secret instinct of our future greatness causes us to look beyond the horizon. But, instead of vain chimeras, the dear mother, without leaving realities, transported her children into a world of enchantment. She showed them heaven, its beauties, the place prepared, the crown promised. She talked to them of the angels, of the Blessed Virgin, and kept these gracious figures before their eyes ; but, above all, she represented to them the child Jesus, the divine model, whose feet and hands they lovingly kissed. Then came the history of the saints and martyrs ; and as nature desires contrasts, in opposition to the open heavens, instead of monsters and phantoms, the mother showed them hell, the invisible enemy who is incessantly prowling for us, and the guardian angel charged with our protection. She insinuated her own sentiments into the minds of the children, who received from her a second life. They loved all that she loved ; what she thought beautiful enchanted them ; when she was affected, their tears flowed, — a wonderful influence, whose extent Madame de Doudeauville fully realized. One might say that she had in herself the destiny of her children.

To preserve their simplicity, and attractive ingenuousness, she would allow neither strangers nor the immediate family to make idols of them, or to notice their words and little ways ; but she accustomed them to be nice to all, cautioning them always to thank those who had done them a kindness. She taught them to do their charities graciously, and to know how to deprive themselves of a gratification in order to have more to give. Their greatest reward was to go to see a poor person, and give him the fruit of some sacrifice. Dreading for them softness and vanity, the ordinary consequences of luxury and well-being, she counteracted these dangerous tendencies by precept and example. She made them understand the necessity of putting themselves aside, and, showing them the crucifix, she taught them gently the merit of suffering, thus preparing happiness for them much more surely than those blind mothers who overload their children with every possible indulgence, under the pretext of making them enjoy at least their early years. These seek to banish any shadow of annoyance, and thus weakened, the children become incapable of bearing the trials which await them. The mother who is truly wise, while blunting the thorn, still allows her child to feel it sometimes. She shows him difficulty, aids, encourages him, and makes him feel the merit and the happiness of winning a victory over himself. It is thus that she fits him for the struggles of life. The beautiful and touching stories of the Old and New Testament served admirably as texts for the teaching of Madame de Doudeauville. These striking pictures of vice and virtue, of rewards and punishments ; these portrayals in glowing colours, the miracles which shine out from the simplicity of the first ages, — all this, while giving a powerful interest to the Bible tales, left an indelible impression upon the mind of the dear children.

It was the mother who received their little confidences. Their joys and griefs, troubles and delights, all were brought to this heart, indulgent without weakness, and they ran quickly to tell her of their naughtiness. She educated their conscience, and was always so patient, so kind, that neither the brother nor sister thought of finding a friend elsewhere. This filial confidence was the safeguard of Mademoiselle Ernestine, who had the happiness to stay under her mother's protection until her marriage. The revolutionary storms obliged Madame de Doudeauville to be separated several times from her son.

Whilst she discharged her maternal duties in this way, she continued her apostolic mission in her husband's family, a mission which, though silent, was not the less active. Her zeal for God consumed her, but her perfect tact made her wait for the favourable moment. Madame de la Rochefoucauld was the first to yield. After admiring her daughter-in-law, she soon came to imitate her, and to associate herself with her heartily in her practices and good works.

Another person soon gave herself up to this happy influence, but for a long time secretly. The Countess of Durtal, at the same time under the spell of virtue and the influence of old prejudices, became the victim of internal conflicts, which the young duchess did not suspect, and of which she was the principal cause. This is what she says of it later : —

"I loved my sister-in-law well, and was much loved by her. I never ceased to pray for her. When we were together, and I saw her adroitly divert the impious or scandalous conversation which she felt was disagreeable to me, I was extremely touched. I longed to show her my gratitude, and to speak to her of God, but was always restrained by the fear of not being skilful enough to meet her objections. I felt, besides, that a conversion of this kind is oftener the effect of an internal touch of grace than of controversy; all of which did not prevent me, however, from writing her long letters, in which I refuted one by one the errors which I had heard her express. I felt myself stronger with my pen than I would have been in conversation;

but as yet I had given her none of this manuscript, when one day she came into my room at five o'clock in the morning. All in tears, she threw herself into my arms, and cried, —

"'I can't hold out; I have n't closed my eyes the whole night; everything in you preaches to me except your words. Why do you never speak to me of God?'

" I took her then to my desk, and putting in her hands the voluminous pages, said, —

"'Read, and judge whether I have thought of you.'"

The ice was broken; there were long talks between the sisters, and when, a few days after, Madame de Doudeauville went to Luchon, she received a letter from her mother-in-law, who announced to her with much happiness, that the countess had approached the sacrament. Madame de Montagu, who was present on the receipt of this good news, saw the face of the duchess suddenly covered with tears.

"What is the matter?" she said, taking her hand.

Madame de Doudeauville imparted her happiness, and the two friends, filled with joy, went to the little neighbouring church to express their gratitude to God. It was a noble victory; for Madame de Durtal, whose soul was brave and generous, giving herself up to piety with fervour, became a model of Christian virtues. Her conversion to religion preceded by only five years her truly heroic death.

The Viscount of Rochefoucauld, harder to gain, had, nevertheless, come to do full justice to his daughter-in-law. He showed her attention, consideration, and even gave her marks of particular confidence. The duchess responded by kindnesses, by zealous little attentions full of delicacy, and she was so successful, that the viscount ended by finding much charm in her society. This happy transformation was to have a result ardently desired by the young woman, and one which the skeptical mind of Monsieur de la Rochefoucauld had allowed her scarcely to hope for. On a sudden a grave malady declares itself; danger becomes imminent; the progress of the disease is so rapid that Monsieur de Doudeauville, on a visit to one of his estates at the time, hastens with all speed to Paris, but arrives only at the last moment; however the family angel was watching by the dying man, and wishing that the father might be united to his children forever. Thanks to her care, the viscount received the last sacraments with full consciousness, and gave evident proofs of faith and of repentance. Before dying he turned to his daughter-in-law, and said, in a trembling voice, " I hope, my dear child, that you are satisfied with me."

In her sorrow the duchess experienced a very sweet consolation; the Lord, in giving her this soul, repaid her generously for the sufferings she had endured in entering

her second family. She mourned her
father-in-law, in whom she had recognized
a heart upright and kind, beneath the de-
lusions of his mind ; but she silenced her
own emotion, to devote herself to the husband, whose grief was so poignant, that
for twenty-four hours he could not collect
himself.

This death, which happened in 1789, left
the affairs of the family household in great
confusion, and left, too, a succession of
enormous debts, due to the bad administration of a steward in whom the viscount had
full confidence. Charged with the conduct
of the affairs of Madame de Doudeauville
as well, in the first year of her married
life, this incapable man had occasioned a
deficit of a hundred thousand francs within
a few months. Justly alarmed at the precipice upon which they were hanging, the
duke and the duchess made a resolve
which proves a determination very rare at
the age of seventeen. Considering all dis-

cussion useless, and all amendment impossible, they confided the care of their property to another man of business chosen by them, who found means to repair the breach without touching their capital. With the same skill, he promptly got into order the estate of the Viscount of Rochefoucauld. The duchess on all these occasions had a sound judgment, and a presence of mind which was remarkable ; her great natural kindness of heart did not prevent her from being firm in a resolution inspired by justice, tending to a good result.

We have spoken of '89, which is to speak of a year of storms. People began to tremble. Some tried to reassure themselves ; but the Duke of Doudeauville, profoundly afflicted, and foreseeing only a fatal issue, had the happy inspiration to separate his own property from that of his wife. His relatives and friends sought in vain to dissuade him from a project in which they saw no advantage to him. To give over to a woman of twenty-five years a revenue of more than a hundred and twenty thousand francs was folly in their eyes. Despite these numerous protests, the duke persisted in his resolution, and thus saved the fortune of his children. He knew well that he could confidently trust the wife and mother.

Being chosen bailiff of Chartres, he had to preside in his office over an assembly of six hundred persons, for the election of the deputies to the States-General. A large faction attempted to break his presidency, protesting against the royal nomination. He stood firm and succeeded in calming their minds ; but what was his embarrassment when, after the opening speech, they demanded that the voting should be per head and not per order, contrary to the instructions given. To triumph over this difficulty, the duke pursued a course which, while it allowed him to remain faithful to his duty, raised neither murmur nor opposition. "Before determining this question," he said, "we must verify our credentials, and must divide in order to hasten the process. The halls are in readiness." Then inviting the nobles to go out with him, and the bishop to march at the head of his clergy, he rose and immediately each one followed his president.

The orders being thus separated, the duke took great care not to bring them together again. Notwithstanding this ingenious manœuvre, the entire assembly returned him a warm vote of thanks ; but not having attained the eligible age for national representative, he could not take a place in the Constituent Assembly.

He was obliged, then, so to speak, to remain a dumb witness of the insane scenes which were the prelude to the bloody catastrophe. Absolutely powerless to stop the revolutionary tide, he decided to go to Italy with all his family.

They went by way of Nice, and he attempted to cross the Var by fording: it was an imprudence; let us listen while he describes this perilous adventure:—

"For several days people had not crossed the river, for the abundant rains had transformed it into a torrent, nearly an eighth of a mile in width; our six horses stopped, unable to stem the force and rapidity of the water, which came into the carriage in quantity. All the efforts of our postilions and guides became useless; the danger was increasing, when I saw on the bank, at a little distance, six post horses which came from Nice. I threw myself on the backs of two men, for one would not have been enough, to go in search of this unexpected succour. The drivers of these horses had to be much coaxed, and yielded to my entreaties only when they saw the gleam of several louis which I promised them, if they would come to our aid; they had, in fact, great trouble to rejoin their carriage.

" It was also most difficult to induce my guides to carry me back to the perilous place from which they had brought me. My wife and children were still there. I wanted to save them, or perish with them ; at last, after the most unheard-of efforts, and by the help of God, we emerged from the torrent ; we arrived soon after at Nice, and thence reached Genoa."

The rank of Spanish grandee gave considerable rights to the titled stranger in this city. He enjoyed the same privileges with the doge; so that it was only necessary to mention his title, and the chains were let down which prevented the passage of carriages in most of the streets. After the hour for closing the gates, he could have them opened, and he profited by this to pass his evenings in the neighboring country-places, where the greater part of the noble families were installed for the fine season. The important personages remaining in Genoa, the senators and sover-

eigns of the country would request the favour of accompanying the young emigrant,
in order to return with him after the regular hour.

This several months' sojourn was marked
by an incident which the perfect discretion
of the good duchess has always concealed,
but which her husband has revealed for the
purpose of doing homage to a virtue such
as one seldom meets with.

The life of pleasure, beneath an enchanting sky, was not without its dangers for a
very active young man of twenty-five, of a
sensitive and impressionable nature. For
lack of serious occupation he sought the
society of agreeable companions, and the
long hours spent with a beautiful Italian
woman ended by so completely charming
him, that he was no longer master of his
imagination. A little more, and his heart
would not have belonged to him.

What must the pious duchess have un-
dergone then ? She has never alluded to

the secret pain which was caused, doubtless, by the change suddenly come over
her husband, and of which she was perfectly conscious ; she did not speak of it ;
but this is what she tells us of this period
of her life : —

"The world," she says, "had upset all
the ideas upon the simple and natural relations of man and God, which I had made
for myself. I was sick at heart for the
perversity and error which I discovered.
It seemed to me that I was participating
in this impiety, and I dared no longer
approach the holy table. Once, my fear
was so great, that while in church I had
almost fainted. I was devoured by scru-
ples, which I could neither analyze nor explain to my confessor. I addressed myself
to a Jesuit father ; happily, he was a judicious man, who never discussed. He cured
me by prescribing for me an act of obedience, which I shall always remember with
emotion. I was then at Genoa, and so

unhappy, because of all that was taking place within me, that, not content with going to confession on the eve of my communions, I returned again in the morning, although I had to go a long distance for it, and I could not always decide to approach the holy mysteries then. One day when I presented myself for a fresh absolution, my confessor, instead of listening, said, addressing me: 'Are you fasting?' 'Yes, my father.' 'Very well; go to the holy table; I will give you communion." I obeyed, trembling, and from that moment my terrors ceased."

It is probable that the suffering of the heart had contributed to augment and to keep up this so painful condition of soul. However that may be, always mistress of herself, and always trusting in the divine protection, the duchess changed in no respect her demeanour towards her husband; she evinced the same tenderness towards him, and if a shade of sadness passed over her face, this tacit reproach was full of sweetness ; it would have roused him who merited it, most certainly, if the fascination of the moment had not, as usual, thrown over the danger the illusion fitted to falsely reassure the conscience, " I shall go no farther."

Madame de Doudeauville had too much good judgment not to see the only remedy needful ; she did not wish to impose it, but proposed it with her ordinary gracefulness.

One day, taking advantage of a letter from her sister who announced the resolution of going abroad, she expressed to her husband the desire to join her. He, deeply moved by the proposition, yielded nevertheless, and in the fear of missing a meeting at Annecy, he did not defer the departure for a moment. But his heart is sick, sad, sorrowful ; he exercises his ennui among the wild and majestic mountains of Savoy, without succeeding in dissipating it ; his wife, not ignorant of the cause of this melancholy, although up to this time she had maintained a silence full of dignity and discretion, now addresses him with a gentle serenity, saying affectionately: "You are troubled; I know it, I see it; why not speak to me? I will share the trouble with you, and may I not, perhaps, lessen it?"

Much touched by these advances, the duke responded, by the most entire confidence; he concealed nothing, and the weight which oppressed his heart painfully, was immediately lightened. "This avowal," he says, "solicited with so much grace and received with so much indulgence, did me good, and reëstablished a little calm in my soul; the result was, that I did not return to Genoa, in accordance with my previous plan."

We understand that one must have established a dwelling higher than the earth, to dare thus to trouble certain waves in order to calm them. Madame de Doudeauville, in the eyes of her husband, as well as of her friends, was placed in a higher sphere, where human passions could not reach her.

A stay of fifteen months in the town of Annecy was pleasant to the exiles, and yet more improving to their piety. The numerous souvenirs left by Saint Francis de Sales in the country and environs, living witnesses of the most ardent charity, impressed the Duke de Doudeauville. He made serious and salutary reflections here; circumstances were favourable to this; the condition of France, the uncertainty and gravity of events, human vicissitudes, this frailty which he could already comprehend and feel, all combined to make him the better appreciate the wisdom of him who had consecrated his life to bringing wandering souls back to God. While praying by this tomb, he felt, in his turn, the desire of loudly declaring his faith. Until then, his natural timidity made him sensitive to pub-

lic opinion. He now adopted the firm resolution to proclaim himself everywhere and
always by faith and practice. The duchess
thanked God for the religious growth of
her husband, and herself tasted the sweets
of a retreat which the noisy festivities of
Genoa made all the more precious to her.
For the trial being past, the soul feels itself
brave and happy ; what it has suffered by
the grace of God, it would at no price cut
out of its life. Hence, while, in following
with interest the phases of an existence
which excites our admiration as much as
our love, we feel by the beating of our
heart, the extent of certain sacrifices, we
would never wish to tear out those pages
where the apogee of glory is reached together with the apogee of suffering.

The noble exiles had put themselves in
communication with the house of Sales,
which kept up some of the pious hospitality
of the holy bishop. Visits became frequent, to the satisfaction of both families,

for it did not take long to recognize the merit of Madame de Doudeauville, as eminent as it was modest.

She also made, in Savoy, the acquaintance of the Abbé of Etyola, to whom she was to render an important service during the French Revolution. This worthy ecclesiastic, seeing her taste for the good and the poor, spoke to her of a most miserable woman, who, although her body was grievously afflicted, was visited by the Lord by sensible favours; for instance, after her communions, when she thought herself alone in the church, she would give thanks, aloud, in a touching way, and she would then say remarkable things, inspired, no doubt, by the Holy Spirit. Madame de Doudeauville went to visit her. Affected by the pitiable condition of this poor creature, who dragged herself about on her knees and elbows, she proposed to cut her nails, which had grown extremely long. The unfortunate woman, looking attentively at her whom her sad fate had so moved, at first held out her hand as if about to accept the service, but she drew it back hastily at the moment when the duchess approached with scissors, and said, in a voice full of expression, " It is enough, you do not despise the poor, the members of Jesus Christ."

After her return to France, Madame de Doudeauville learned with pleasure from the Abbé d'Etyola, that this holy woman had prayed for her before her death.

The short rest at Annecy, the repose in prayer and in the peaceful contemplation of the beauties of nature, these were a preparation for the great struggles for which every quarter of France seemed already to have given the signal.

In the beginning of the year 1792, the Duke of Doudeauville took his way back to Paris, where he wished to wind up some affairs, and to inform himself of the state of men's minds. His wife, full of the desire to follow him, had begged him to ask his friends if it would not be possible to return ; the general opinion being favourable, they quitted foreign soil. But Monsieur de Doudeauville, in spite of his dislike of emigration, carried away by the hope of saving the king and freeing his country from a hateful tyranny, soon separated himself from all that he held most dear. With death in his soul, he bade farewell to all his own, and betook himself to the banks of the Rhine, to put his sword for a time at the service of a cause which he believed would bring deliverance to his country. But after a first sad campaign, when he perceived that the powers in league concealed ambitious designs under the avowed project of delivering the king and restoring order to France, he left the army and condemned himself to a weary waiting.

CHAPTER IV.

DURING THE REVOLUTION.

THE Duchess of Doudeauville, whom the applause of the court left indifferent, and who remained calm, humble, and consequently strong in prosperity, is now ready to meet the perils of the revolution. The events which are about to bring her in contact with difficulties of every kind, will reveal to us how much courage and heroic charity is contained in a heart where God has established his reign. Faithful to her mission, we shall see her always prudent, but yet more devoted, forgetting her own danger to sustain those belonging to her, to succour the unhappy, and to defend the interests of religion wherever there is opportunity.

At all times, when she is at liberty, we

see her by the bed-side of the sick, at the prison door ; she finds the priest and ac-companies him to the dying ; she saves the holy eucharist from profanation, even at the peril of her life. Thus, she receives one day from the hands of a priest, who has just administered the last sacraments, and fears that he may be arrested, the Pyx in which are several consecrated frag-ments ; full of respect, she carries it away and places it lovingly in her prie-Dieu, where she has already been permitted to preserve a wafer to communicate herself in danger of death. In spite of the diffi-culty of the times, she found means of having the Blessed Sacrifice celebrated in her house nearly every day.

She learns that at the Visitation, Rue du Bac, after having imprisoned the chaplain, they had affixed seals to the tabernacle, while waiting for the priest, who had taken the civic oath. Profoundly affected at the thought of a profanation, in order to avoid it, she proposes removing the reserved sacrament at her own risk and peril. The superior, while praising her zeal, refuses ; for even if she had consented to expose herself personally, she could not compromise, as she must infallibly have done, the virtuous duchess and all the nuns.

In vain is the sentence of death pronounced against those who give an asylum to the faithful priests. Madame de Doudeauville conceals in her house a German ecclesiastic, and as considerate as she is generous, she desires that the Abbe Vinclimput should not know the price at which he received his kind hospitality ; but a servant in the secret, fearful, no doubt, for his mistress, and a little for himself, warns the good priest, who exclaims : "I should be wretched if my stay here should expose the respected people to whom I owe everything." Notwithstanding the solicitation of the good duchess, he changed his asylum at once ; he is arrested the next day, and mounts the scaffold.

Madame de Doudeauville could not be forgotten. On the 28th of May, 1793, whilst she is assisting at mass with her mother-in-law, and Madame Durtal, they tell her that the red bonnets are coming in by the court-yard gate. She rises promptly, goes in advance of them, and leading them to the garden, keeps their attention until the end of the Blessed Sacrifice. When she judges there has been time for the priest to escape, she enters the house with her dismal visitors ; being immediately arrested by them, as well as Madame de la Rochefoucauld and the countess, her sister-in-law, she is conducted to a house in the Rue de Sèvres, which served for barracks the night before. As she is about to enter, Mademoiselle Ernestine, then eleven years old, throws herself into her mother's arms, and refuses to be separated from her ; but they tear her away with violence, and the tears and supplications of the poor child do not obtain for her permission even to come to see her from whom she had never been separated. Her despair rends the mother heart, without shaking a courage raised above human attack. Madame de Doudeauville leaves to her daughter, with her blessing, a reassuring word, and surmounting her own suffering, she tries to alleviate the grief of her companions. They are all three put in one ruinous room, where four miserable straw mattresses comprise the furniture. The courageous duchess immediately takes two, putting one on top of the other, and makes her mother and sister-in-law sit down, lavishing on them the most eager care.

Quite absorbed in making this abode less painful, she asks and obtains for them a few comforts; and her kindness and virtue make such an impression upon their guards, that when, after a detention of eight days, the noble prisoners are set at liberty, there is a general rejoicing.

But Mademoiselle Ernestine tastes but

for a little while the happiness of being
with her mother again. These ladies, arrested the second time, are subjected to an
imprisonment, less rigourous, but longer
than the first. For two months they had
to undergo visits, searching, questionings ;
to hear denunciations, threats of death ;
and all these called forth the brightness of
Madame de Doudeauville's virtue, without
once shaking it : sweet and patient, she
was at the same time firm and dignified ;
they respected while they admired her.

One night, having thrown a little water
out of the window, before going to bed, she
hears directly a racket all about her room ;
the guard are alarmed. "What can that
extraordinary noise be," say they ; "without
doubt the prisoner has passed out some
conspirator's letter." It seems, indeed, as
if the country may be in danger ! They
knock at her door, she gets up, opens it,
and answers quietly, — "Go and look, my

7

friends." Out of countenance, they retire, and leave her to sleep in peace.

On regaining her liberty, she availed of it to occupy herself with her children, and to carry aid to numerous sufferers. She thought to have breathed freely for awhile with her mother and sister-in-law, but these two ladies, three days after their deliverance, are again arrested and shut up this time with some English nuns, become themselves absolute prisoners in their convent. What contributed to save Madame de Doudeauville, on this occasion, was precisely what should have lost her. Being interrogated at length about her husband, she answered with the most loyal frankness ; to the invectives launched against the emigrant, she responded, by taking up his defence most spiritedly, for all the repeated signs from her mother-in-law, who trembled at her rashness.

" You are then afflicted at his absence ? " they said.

" Yes, certainly."

" Then you miss him ? "

" Very much."

" Well, citizen, I see you are a good woman ; we will do you no harm."

And the next day, in fact, when the section heard the report of the interrogatory, instead of condemning, it applauded this courageous frankness.

The wish to fulfil at the same time her duty towards her daughter, her sister, and her mother, inspired the generous duchess with the idea of going with her Ernestine to board in this community of English ladies where her dear relatives were staying. The superior received her with open heart ; but scarcely was she installed, when a new and yet more terrible misfortune fell upon the prisoners.

The hour of great sacrifices is for the true Christian the hour of heroic virtues. If nature, trembling as the cup of bitterness approaches, attempts to put it from

the lips, and utters that cry which escaped from the tenderest love, "Let it
pass from me," grace adds after the example, and through the strength of the Divine Saviour, "Not my will, but Thine be
done." Happy the soul which loses neither
faith nor trust in time of trial.

On the 8th of March, 1794, the Countess
of Durtal, summoned to appear before the
revolutionary tribunal, tears herself from
her mother's embrace, and goes to receive
calmly the sentence of death. Conducted
to the Conciergerie, she meets there Monsieur de l'Aigle, her uncle, the involuntary
author of her arrest. Admirable design
of Providence! While the count groans,
not over his own fate, but that of a young
woman whom he has compromised by an
insignificant letter found upon her writing-
table, she, sublime in her courage and piety,
profiting by the few hours that remain, becomes the apostle of the condemned noble-
man; happy to buy, by the shedding of her

own blood, the happiness of bringing a soul to God. She showed herself so admirable up to the very last moment, that her guard, affected, prayed with her; one of them was converted, and averred that he had never seen so beautiful a death.

These details were a consolation to Madame de Doudeauville, who had made fabulous efforts to force her way to the Conciergerie. She was losing a sister, a sweet companion, whom a conformity of religious feeling had made peculiarly dear for five years. She was feeling, keenly, too, the grief of her mother-in-law; but the thought of eternal reunion gave to her resignation a something which was really celestial.

She learned soon after, with emotion, that her uncle, the Marshal of Mouchy-Noailles, in going to execution, had first pronounced these words of a hero and martyr: "At the age of eighteen I mounted to the assault for my king; at eighty, I can well mount the scaffold for my God!"

Things went on very fast in those times, and it was not possible for friendship to pour the balm of consolation upon the deepest griefs, in peace. Madame de Doudeauville sustained the Viscountess de la Rochefoucauld after the death of her daughter; these ladies hoped that they need no more be parted, and now a decree of the Convention obliges all of the nobility who are not prisoners to leave the capital. This was a fresh stab for these two women, each of whom seemed indispensable to the other; and yet it was not a subject of deliberation. The courageous duchess owed herself before everything to her husband and children; in remaining voluntarily in Paris, she would compromise an existence which belonged no more to herself. They separated then, notwithstanding the heartbreakings. Always in presence of the divine will, in which she read every event, Madame de Doudeauville accepted with equal submission good and ill, and she knew how to communicate this feeling admirably to those who had to do with her. Recommending her mother-in-law to the superior of the community, she left her resigned, and disposed to await better days.

But in order to get away, it was necessary to ask a passport, and for this, she needed nine witnesses. In order to procure these witnesses, the good duchess who knew nobody in the quarter where the convent was, addresses herself to the gardener, who brings her the nine sureties the next day. Being arrived at the court of hearing, she finds a poor blind nun the object of universal mockery ; she approaches her kindly, asks about the business which brings her there, and seeing in her hand a paper needing a signature, she leads her to the clerk's office, and so delivers her from the public ridicule. . . . . Patiently she is going to wait for her own turn, when a witness of her act of charity says to the officer : " I hope you will allow this citizen to pass who has been here for three or four hours." Then they ask her quality. " Ex-noble," she answers. The questioner, who wishes to save her, says quickly, in a low voice : " Say, instead, living on your income." She understands and repeats after him the assertion which in no wise compromises her conscience.

The president, touched by her honesty, takes her name, her address, and giving her his own, begs her in any need, to have recourse to him. " It was," she says, simply, " my beauty and my youth which made him interest himself for me."

Withdrawn to the little village of Wissous, four leagues from Paris, she continues her truly apostolic life, all the time watching over the education of her children. Several nuns of the Visitation, driven from their convent, found with her an open hospitality, the retirement, and almost the regularity of the cloister. Mesdames de Barnage and de Noland take pleasure in giving lessons to Mademoiselle Ernestine, and in fitting her to receive her first communion. When the dear child has reached her twelfth year, they transform her mother's room into a chapel, and then, privately, takes place in a simple and touching way, the greatest act of her life. They had to surround themselves with precautions, to escape all eyes ; but the holy duchess had good and faithful servants, on whom she could count.

During her sojourn at Wissous, Madame de Doudeauville learns that a new-born baby in the village is running a great risk of not receiving baptism, because the parents know of no faithful priest. She goes to the family instantly, proposes her daughter Ernestine for god-mother, and asks them to trust the interesting little creature to her for a moment. When by her care the waters of baptism have made of it a child of God, she kisses it with tenderness, and while giving it back to the mother, watches over her little protégée from afar.

This kiss, this blessing of a saint, can but bring the child happiness. After the death of her daughter, the pious duchess, engrossed with doing in her name and to her memory, the greatest possible good, will not forget her who was held over the baptismal font. Well brought up, and afterwards respectably married, the second Ernestine will show herself worthy of her benefactress, who, to her dying day is to count among her chiefest joys the prosperity of a family whose happiness she made. She will receive from this family such sincere tokens of gratitude, as that she will require to be consoled for getting her recompense here below.

As long as a civic priest officiated in the parish of Wissous, the duchess never appeared, but went to hear a mass said privately by Monsieur de Bonnatier, in the house of Madame de Lucy. But so soon as a faithful pastor came back to the little village church, she betook herself there with

all speed, and gave ornaments and vases
for the altar, that there might be no delay
in celebrating the holy offices worthily.

It was at the altar that she sought the
strength and consolation which she needed
to endure a painful suspense. In almost
complete ignorance of the fate of her husband, she often asked herself if he might
not be in need of the necessaries of life.
At his departure, she had given him the
silver plate and her diamonds, but, might
not the fruits of their sale be already spent?
Did he know of the death of his sister?
The imprisonment of his mother? Without an answer to the thousand questions
called forth by a tenderness so justly
alarmed, she confided her grief to the God
of her heart, who, while He caused her to
pass through trial, had always marvellously
sustained her.

One day, after renewing her act of faith,
she finds that a good man has arrived, de-
puted by the Duke de Doudeauville, to fetch

her as well as the children. The measures are well taken, he says. By means of a disguise, she is to pass for his relative, and will so cross the frontier. With what eagerness does the duchess ask news of the poor exile. What has become of him? What does he know? Any exchange of letters would have gravely endangered the messenger, and it is from his lips that she learns the sad regrets of the brother, and the anxiety of the father and husband. This is how Monsieur de Doudeauville had known the death of his sister.

"One day," he says, "at Aix la Chapelle, as I was reading aloud, according to my custom, the English and French newspapers in a reading-room, my hearers saw me suddenly turn pale, tremble, and presently faint. I had read out of the corner of my eye, under the article, Paris, these three lines: "The citizen Durtal, and the citizen de l'Aigle were executed yesterday, in the Place of the Revolution." It was like being struck by lightning. My sister, whom I had loved so tenderly! She was a widow, and if they had killed her, I said to myself, would they not also kill the wife, the mother of the emigrant? My existence became a perpetual torture, or rather, I ceased to live; the post days, which I awaited with a mortal impatience, brought me terrible agony. I thought to find in each line of the paper the condemnation of those who were so dear to me. How does one survive such anxiety?

"An excellent friend of Madame de Doudeauville, on learning this tragic event and my cruel position, left Brussels with her husband in a kind of cart, the only carriage which their limited means allowed them, and they both came to bring me the one consolation which friendship can offer — the weeping and praying together."

This excellent friend was the Marchioness of Montagu, a truly admirable woman, who was soon to hear that her mother, grandmother, and sister had just swollen the number of the heroic victims of the revolution.

After some days of agony, the Duke of Doudeauville, trembling for his wife and children, had trusted to a brave Swiss the mission of bringing them to him. There was needed for this a sum which was considerable in proportion to the financial condition of the exile. He divided with his mother-in-law, the Marchioness of Montmirail, who had taken refuge in England, a modest income of four thousand five hundred francs ; but, what were all privations compared with the perspective of this sword constantly suspended over the heads which he would fain have saved at the price of his blood ?

Madame de Doudeauville, ready to brave all perils if she might rejoin her husband, made herself ready to start ; but with her customary considerateness, before entering upon the journey, she inquires whether her

departure can expose anybody to danger.
Her devoted servants assure her they
fear nothing, and, if it were necessary,
would give their lives to save hers ; but
her landlord, on being informed, far from
using the same language, declares that
the consequences of the flight will fall
upon him, and that if Madame de Doudeauville leaves his house, he will denounce
her. She is obliged consequently to give
up the journey.

A little while after, this courageous
woman, impelled by her generous zeal, exposed herself to the most serious danger.

The Abbé of Etyola, whom she had
known at Annecy, being at Bordeaux, in the
thickest of the revolution, is arrested there
just as he is about to embark for the Brit-
ish Isles ; the devoted duchess hears that
he has been detained, and that the plan is
to take him to Guyane. She writes in a
hurry to a person of her acquaintance, beg-
ging her to hasten and deliver the good

abbé, giving him in her name three thousand francs. This unsigned note, being taken to the Hotel de Mouchy, is found there during a domiciliary visit. Madame de Doudeauville learns the fact; immediately she calls a faithful servant and begs him to accompany her to the revolutionary tribunal. "But you don't think of doing that, madame," answers the terrified man. He had to follow her. Being arrived, she leaves Arnolet at the door, and presents herself, alone, for a hearing before the terrible Fouquier-Tainville. He pays no attention to her; standing for two hours, she waits, motionless, until compatriots and friends have retired. Then, tête-à-tête with the accuser-general, she says to him :—

"I have an important affair to communicate to you."

"My only business is to punish the enemies of the republic. What have you to say? This is the place for making denunciations."

"It is exactly a denunciation which brings me."

"Very good ; speak citizen."

"I am about to make such an one as you are not accustomed to hear ; it is myself, and myself alone whom I denounce."

"It is death that you come to meet."

"I know ; but I am fulfilling a duty."

He looks at her with surprise, and listens attentively. She relates her history in all its details, but without naming anybody, and ends by saying: "If there be anybody to prosecute it is I." The fierce revolutionist answers with stupefaction: "Do you know that I have feeling, too ? Why do you interest yourself for this priest ?"

"Because he is unfortunate."

"Ah, yes, I understand, and I have a heart ; I have saved a good many people."

He reassures her, promising that nobody shall be prosecuted ; and seeing her pale and trembling with fatigue, he offers

8

her his arm as far as the stairway. This bare arm, which seemed stained with the blood of numerous and innocent victims, prompted a repulsive movement from the poor woman, easy to understand. As it was offered in kindness, she could not decline, but she shuddered always at the recollection of the support accepted for those few seconds.

On leaving Fouquier-Tainville, she tells him her name and address, so that he might find her in case of need. He assures her again that the case is ended. The Abbé d'Etyola is released, in fact, receives the three thousand francs, and crosses to England. Shortly after, being returned to Annecy, with the title of bishop, he wrote to his liberator, and, to testify his gratitude, sent her a reliquary containing a joint of the finger of Saint François de Sales, and of Saint Chantal; he knew that nothing could be more acceptable.

The feeling of having a duty to discharge,

or a service to render, gave intrepid courage to this delicate and sensitive woman.
Opportunity discovered in her a strength of
will, a firmness of character, which, always
joined to the greatest modesty, ended by
triumphing over every difficulty.

Her estates having been put into seques-
tration, she insists upon her rights, and
energetically defends her interests, which
are the interests of her children and the
poor as well. Having learned that they intended to sell the furniture of the Château
de Montmirail, under the pretext that the
husband being an emigrant, half the common property should be confiscated for
the good of the state, she went in haste,
proved that she was married under the
system of separate marriage settlements,
and had justice done her.

Always kind to her own, she joyfully
welcomed the Viscountess of Rochefoucauld, who hurried back to her after a year
of captivity. She often visited her sister,

Madame de Montesquiou, who, amid so many subjects for alarm, had the sorrow to lose a charming little girl, so pious and charitable, that she wanted to give all her clothes to cover poor children. Rozamée was very fond of her Aunt de Doudeauville. A relative, in taking leave of her, having said one day, "What would you like me to bring back to you from Paris?" The dear child had answered quickly, "Bring me back my aunt."

The good God called this little angel to him at the age of eight years. She thought she was going to heaven, but did not wish to cause sorrow to her mother; so, feeling herself about to die, she said to her: "Go away, mamma, I am going to sleep." The poor mother went away, and the child never awoke. Madame de Doudeauville, at the news of this death, went from Wissous to Maupertuis in a cart, to comfort her sister. In wiping away her tears, she little thought that in a few years she was about to weep over the most loving and loved of daughters.

About this time, happily, she confided to the Abbé Legris-Duval the education of her son Sosthènes, who, up to that time, through a succession of circumstances due to the misfortunes of the times, had had only indifferent masters. The new teacher, equally distinguished for his qualities of mind and heart, attached his young pupil to him, and became the devoted friend of the entire family, which he did not again leave, and whose sorrows and joys he shared. "He was, until his death," says the Duke of Doudeauville, "the delight and the edification of our home."

The virtuous duchess did not limit her zealous efforts to the family circle, and persons of the household. When she saw a soul which ignorance or contact with impiety had plunged in gloom, she suffered, and sought every opportunity to make it know and taste the truth; it was rare that she was resisted.

Madame Helvétius, after the death of a daughter, fell into a profound languor ; her friends tried in vain to attach her to life, and as religion was a closed book to her, she knew not where to rest her heart. Her state inspired Madame de Trans with a warm interest, and she saw her often, but not daring to speak the language of faith herself, she sent a nun from time to time, to ask after her health. She hoped that the good sister would find an opening to slip in a word about God for the poor sufferer, but the door of the sick-room was always closed against her, and the most frightful solitude continued to reign in the heart which, lacking hope, was also comfortless. This double calamity, in time and eternity, profoundly touched Madame de Doudeauville, to whom Madame de Trans confided her vain endeavours. Immediately she proposed to go to see Madame Helvétius herself, dressed as a maid ; and without delay she finds the house. She knocks, gives the

name of her whom she represents, and expresses her wish to see the invalid. They
hesitate, are even on the point of sending
her away, but the half-open door has permitted Madame Helvétius to follow the
little debate between her custodian and the
messenger of her friend. The sweet voice
and the discreet language wherein a great
interest is manifest, inspires her with a will-
ingness to see the visitor; she asks to
have her shown into the room, bids her sit
down, inspects her, is astonished, and rec-
ognizes that it is not a maid with whom
she has to do. They enter into conversation; the pious duchess approaches the
subject of her grief with exquisite delicacy.
She understands, she feels, she wishes
to alleviate. . . . . The sick woman, who
knows her noble visitor by reputation, has
soon guessed her personality, and strongly
moved, she cries: "You are Madame de
Doudeauville! She only can talk like this."
Then begins intimacy; feeling herself un-

derstood, she whom sadness overwhelms gives free vent to her tears, to her regrets; the thought of God, as the true and only comforter, is not repelled; it is still something that is very vague to a poor soul so long lost in error; but this first interview leaves a sweet impression with her, and a charm until then unknown. They agree to see each other again, and little by little daylight comes, light grows stronger, grace more urgent. Madame de Doudeauville speaks of confession, and herself finds an ecclesiastic fitted for this office. The interesting convert has such confidence in her new and holy friend, that she offers to make an avowal of her faults to her, before telling the priest. Having found faith, peace, and hope, Madame Helvétius continues to see Madame de Doudeauville, for whom she cherishes a gratitude which may be called eternal.

And now the horizon grown less black· in France, allowed one to begin to breathe there. In the beginning of 1797, the efforts of the coalition were no longer to be feared. Bonaparte restored to the armies their ancient prestige, and already the foreign powers humbly sued for peace.

In the interim, the nation, restored to itself, burned with desire to wipe off the stain of blood with which its brow was stained in the gloomy days of '93. This awakening of France was specially apparent when a deputy, on the very day when he entered the Cinq-Cents, solicited liberty for the Catholic religion, and the abolition of the laws directed against the clergy. His motion was listened to without anger, warmly supported by some, and on the 24th of August, 1797, the Chamber voted for the new decree.

These were solemn proofs of a better future. A few took advantage of this to cross the frontier and see their relatives and exiled friends. The courageous duchess left Paris no later than the 31st of

August, in the same year, and undertook a long journey, of which the account is given us by Mademoiselle Ernestine, then fifteen years old.

"There are circumstances in life, my dear cousin, when one can neither talk with those he loves, nor write to them; but I feel sure that there are none which prevent his thinking of them."

"If misfortunes are softened by the tender attentions of friendship, joy shared by it is even more delicious. Judge, then, how much I need you at this moment, to open my heart to you. A witness of my sorrows, why can you not be of my happiness? I wish, at least, to describe to you all that I have seen, thought, and felt.

"We left Paris, as you know, on Wednesday, the 31st of August, at four o'clock in the morning. My little note must have showed you that if my mind was not quite awake, at least my sentiment for you has never slumbered.

"I will not attempt to picture to you the emotions that agitated my heart at the moment of departure. I was about to see again a father whom I had left when a little child, but for whom I had cherished the tenderest feelings. You know that his absence became more painful to me in proportion as my age made me better understand and feel it.

"Our guide did not reach the first post station until an hour and a half after us. Oh, how long the time seemed to me. Different thoughts were suggested by my imagination. I didn't know what to attribute this delay to, and the fear of seeing our journey fall through, passed quickly from my head to my heart. I saw happiness elude me at the very moment I was about to seize it. At last we perceived the carriage. We were soon consoled for our long waiting, for whilst we were lamenting, they had been mending a wheel, which would have broken in a short time, spilling

us out, I don't know where. There is reason in saying that a small evil is often the
cause of a great good. The next morning
at nine o'clock we were at Auxerre, where
we were to have slept the night before. To
remedy the delay, and regain that wretched
time, which, according to Sosthènes, will
always get lost, it was agreed that we
should spend the next night on the road.
We stopped for supper, however, for my
mother thought that, as we had had no
dinner, it was best to make one meal a
day.

" I shall not be able to mention all the
places through which we passed, but must
at least tell you how we had to cross for-
ests, whose sombre look made me shiver,
which woke me up a little. Arrived at
Auxonne in the night, they would not give
us horses. After a pretty lively dispute,
we had recourse to the municipal officers,
who interfered in our favor, happily, and
we set out at last, led by postilions in a
very bad humor.

" Hardly do we leave the town when we perceive three men following our carriage ; then, of a sudden, they leave us, and run after the other, already at some distance. What a fright ! It is night ; we are in a very solitary spot, and as fear magnifies objects, I charitably informed my mother that we were then in the midst of a wood. There was n't the vestige of one. . . . . For all that, I was n't the only frightened one. Judge of the situation of your cousin who fears robbers in the heart of Paris, in a well-closed house, and who now finds herself in the open fields, guided by dissatisfied postilions, and in a carriage where are only women. Sosthènes was in the other, for surely, if he had been in ours, we should not have been allowed to be frightened.

" After all we had only the apprehension without the evil. At Dôle, new obstacles awaited us ; the gates were closed, and we were forced to resign ourselves to passing the night at an inn outside of the town. It was one o'clock. Consequently, we found everybody in bed and asleep. A girl came and opened the door to us, however, with a bad enough grace, and as the rooms were taken, she lodged us in a pretty narrow passage, where four dirty beds were ranged in a row, with their heads against the wall, like a hospital, and we were very glad of this fine palace. With our candle on the floor, for want of a table, and our two chairs, for four people, we were better off than in the street.

"Monsieur Filietaz took Sosthènes into his room, which was much more beautiful, but, as it would seem, not a great deal cleaner, for the next day, when he came into our carriage, my brother brought us an insect which I do not care to name, but of the most unpleasant kind.

"At half past three they make us get up in order to start at five, and I give myself up to sorrow for losing, unnecessarily, this time from sleep. We soon reach Poligny, —the first town of the Jura. I cannot describe to you the impression made upon me by this grand country, with its majestic mountains. Now there are only jagged rocks, frightful precipices, impetuous torrents, gigantic pines which seem to reach the sky; then, without transition, are prairies covered with flocks, with huts, and even cultivated fields.

"Although Morez is not the extreme frontier, it is the place where the Customhouse does its office. So we had to show everything that we had. When they had examined and seen all, they put leaden seals upon our parcels; with this precaution, and the payment of a few crowns, they allowed us to pass on quietly. Hardly had we crossed the French boundary when Monsieur Filietaz got down from his carriage, and came to tell us with the greatest feeling, that we were in Switzerland. I could not contain myself for joy, and I thought I saw on all the faces of the good Swiss the impress of my happiness. Soon we perceived Nyon. We had a small hope of finding my father there. We stopped at the inn, where Madame Filietaz awaited her husband; but even before embracing her, he came to tell us that the person whom we expected was not there. And much more attentive to our interests than to his own, he found horses which could take us on immediately to Lausanne. Unhappily, a fine gentleman, named Prévost, appeared, who, while saying how sensitive he was, stated in a way that was not at all so, that we ought n't to dream of starting that day, because we should n't arrive until midnight, and should have to wake up my father. My mother made up her mind to this inconvenience; but Monsieur Prévost pretended that our nocturnal arrival would be the town talk, which would be very compromising. This reason decided everything, and it was arranged that we should not leave until the next day, at daybreak. I was very angry with this sensitive Monsieur Prévost, who retarded our happiness so pitilessly. Finally, the longed-for morning came, and after being on the road for a few leagues, we perceived Lausanne ; arrived at the gates, we left the carriage, and Monsieur Prévost made us cross through a part of the town without saying whether we were getting any nearer. He made us climb a very dark stairway up to the fourth story, preserving a profound silence all the time. Then he opened a little door, disappeared, and I found myself in my father's arms.

"Must I try to tell you what I felt ? No ; your heart is too delicate not to guess. And, besides, to describe such sentiments would be to weaken them."

The enjoyment was, indeed, very sweet, on both sides. "The happiness which this reunion gave me," says Monsieur de Doudeauville, "was beyond all description. We

9

had been separated for five years, and I had almost despaired of our meeting.

"I passed my days luxuriating in the marvellous change of my situation, in listening to the recital of the sufferings and the alarms of my dear travellers, in hearing the details of all that wisdom, courage, and tenderness had inspired a good mother to do for the welfare of our children.

"I was never tired of hearing them repeat what they had already told me, and even what I knew before their arrival ; my thoughts had been so constantly turned towards France and my absent family. And now I had eyes, ears, and heart, only to seize, understand, and make my own, so to speak, that past in which I had had no part."

At the end of two months they were obliged to part again, for the presence of Madame de Doudeauville was indispensable to the preservation of her numerous estates, and her husband could not put his foot on French soil without danger. They said their sad good-byes. But in spite of all his resolutions to wait for a signal, the poor emigrant could not hold out for long, and soon, aided by the passport of a Swiss merchant, braving a thousand dangers, thanks to skilful stratagems and the now often used currency of daring, he arrives at Orléans, where he reads aloud before a large audience in a book-shop, this article in a paper : "The sentence of death is pronounced anew against every emigrant, and if he be recognized, he shall be shot in twenty-four hours' time."

More alarmed than content, the good duchess hastens to greet her husband, whose extreme tranquillity reassures her at first. But two days after, hearing that he has been denounced to the police, she begs and conjures him to depart. . . . . It is impossible to resist her entreaty. She gives the poor traveller a book of Saint François de Sales, to console him on the way. Wearied with so great emotion, she dreams of making a retreat, and consecrates ten days to repose, under the eye of the Lord. That she may be the quieter, she goes every morning to the Convent of the Filles-Dieu, near the Saint-Denis gate, and does not come back to her little family until the evening. . These hours of solitude recall to her those which were associated with her first communion; a mingling of holy desires, of delicious transports, of prophetic warnings, and of pious resignation. Many years have passed since, and now, in the strength of age, in presence not of a simple presentiment, but with the full understanding of sacrifice, this generous soul renews the giving of her entire self, asking of God in return, that His reign should come, that He should be known, loved, and glorified. As if to show that her offering is accepted, the Holy Spirit inspires the superior of the convent to give her as a souvenir of the retreat, a precious relic of the true cross and of the holy crown of thorns.

A serious thought then occupied Madame de Doudeauville; she began to consider about determining the future of her daughter, who had just entered her seventeenth year. The uncertainty of events doubtless contributed to her making this hasty resolution; not being able to foresee how much longer the head of the family would be kept away, she looked about for a protector outside of the family for the beloved daughter from whom she would fain never have been separated. But before trusting her to other hands, she drew out for her some written counsels, where we see with the mother's tenderness, the ardent and enlightened faith of the strong Christian. These counsels seem to us so wise that we do not fear to reproduce them entire; first, because they may serve for example and instruction, but also because they will make known her who dictated them better than anything which we could say. She advises nothing that she has not practised herself in a much higher degree. The reflections which she inculcates in her daughter were the habitual nourishment of her soul. The sentiments with which she desires to animate her filled her own heart and directed her every action. It is thus that she loved God and her neighbor, with this difference, that she gives of her plenitude what a prudent discretion induces her to impose upon others, with reserve ; knowing no time, no repose in the exercise of virtue, she went on always growing in humility and charity.

These counsels are addressed to an intelligent young girl, spirited, generous, zealous, admirably gifted for the family and too well for the world, perfectly brought up, but whose accomplishments, — I had almost said whose qualities, — are a danger, as the fears expressed by her mother indicate : so true is it that it is not enough that God

and those who represent Him should work
directly for our sanctification : it is a personal work ; it must be that it cost us
something ; and the more the Lord has
given, the more will He ask.

CHAPTER V.

"You will think it singular, my dear Ernestine, that, having you always under my eye, I should still think it necessary to write to you. But I know that you will have as great pleasure in receiving marks of my engrossing interest in you, as I have desire to multiply them. My advice, my counsels, which your heart always appreciates, even when they oppose its tastes and inclinations, will have, I am sure, yet more value if they are written. There are some, besides, which I have reserved for a more advanced age, and the new estate which you are about to enter induces me to communicate them to you.

"I am about to open my heart to you, then, to let you see the hopes which are given me by all that God has done in you, the virtues which I have a right to expect from the germs which rejoiced me in your infancy, and also from the qualities which a great elevation of sentiment, joined to happy gifts of intelligence, should cultivate to a high degree in you. I shall not conceal from you my apprehensions, while preferring that you should not suspect their full extent; for you are not yet a mother; you would not be able to understand all the happiness and pain, the delights and anxieties that this feeling brings.

" I will also make my confession to you : it is necessary to my repose. I am far from attributing to you, my child, the faults that I find in you; it is the small experience I had when I began your education; it is my own shortcomings that I accuse, — above all my small virtue which held back God's blessings from you. With this conviction, judge how important I feel it to fortify you against the dangers which alarm me, and pardon me if I exaggerate a little. See only the tender sentiment of a Christian mother, who trembles at the moment of separation from a cherished daughter. Imagine a merchant, trusting to the sea his treasure, the fruit of his watchings, of his toils, his only hope. He beholds at the same time the haven where he would wish to see it enter, and the innumerable perils which may prevent. He hears on all sides the noise of the waves that may engulf it; picture to yourself his agitation, his torture, and you will have an imperfect idea of the anguish and perplexities of your mother. One only thought has power to calm her, and therefore, I return to it incessantly; it is that of the religious principles which I have always known to be in you, and the liveliness of your faith. I will not say your piety, for I do not think that that name should be given to your actual way of life; but if you persevere, this precious gift will be granted to you for a recompense, and will make the road easy where you are already walking.

"My one desire is, that you should accustom yourself to sound practice, without which your faith would soon grow weak. The world and its friends would exercise their empire over you ; their maxims would not seem so strange to you ; little by little they might please and end by seducing you. Regard for public opinion, which has already made some impression upon you, would hasten your overthrow. . . . . I pause, my child, and can bear no longer the sight of such a misfortune ; the way to avoid it is to animate your faith by the study of our holy religion. Apply yourself to understand what she asks of you, and what she promises to you. I feel the more earnestness, my child, in encouraging you to enter upon this research, because it will occupy you with the only method of finding lasting happiness, and of obtaining it for all who will be dependent upon you.

Without her heavenly succour, you may, it
is very true, have moments of enjoyment
and of pleasure, and you may cause others
to feel them, but the difference! And how
dearly you would pay for these short sea-
sons of illusion! Your enjoyments would
never be without anxiety, nor your pleasures without remorse. The happiness of
which I speak, and which religion offers
to you, since it has its source in purity of
heart, and in the peace of soul which is
the happy result, can never be troubled by
events nor circumstances. It will spread
a charm over all your life. The world may
be overthrown, empires destroyed, men
may tear each other asunder, but there is
no human power which can take from us
this precious gift, and having it we can
bear all. It is not only the impression of
a sentiment which makes me use this language to you, it is the fruit of my experience. May I be able to communicate to
your soul the convictions which I have

drawn from it. Whoever has gone through the French revolution and survived it, can no longer doubt the nothingness of the things of this earth. I have seen honours, titles vanish away, and with them those who wore them; the greatest and best secured fortunes have been annihilated; great names trailed in the mud; brilliant reputations tarnished; the most useful institutions have come to naught. At last the throne and the altar were thrown down; this fine dream with which I had seen men intoxicated, to which they had sacrificed their health, their repose, their conscience; eight years later it had no existence.

" In this total overthrow has not my soul had reason to cry aloud more than once, ' Thou alone art great, O my God. Thou only art stable. Thou alone meritest that we should love Thee above all. Thou only canst promise and give us a lasting happiness. All human supports on which I stayed myself have crumbled away. Thou only remainest to me; but with this firm prop I can endure all.'

" Give, then, to God, and undividedly, the first years at your disposal. Thanks be to heaven, your infancy was consecrated to Him. Consecrate to Him also your youth, and do not question the liberality with which this God of goodness will reward your sacrifices and encourage your first steps. Once in the way where He would have you, He will take care Himself to level the obstructions which you may find there, and will make easy for you the second part of the precept, the love of your neighbour, for then you will everywhere love and respect His work, but how especially in the unfortunate, the needy, in that portion of humanity which is stripped of all temporal advantages and under which He presents Himself to you, while He waits to compensate it liberally one day for the neglect of men. What will you not render to the Lord for that He has put into

your hands a means so simple and so precious of expiating the faults inseparable
from the enjoyment of a large fortune, and
of getting your pardon while all the time
yielding to the gentle inclination of your
heart. In your superiors you will see the
authority of God, and the submission, the
consideration which you owe them, will
become easy to you.

"With your inferiors your manner of
command will not be severe ; your rule
will be one of kindness. Impartiality with
all carefulness being your law, prejudice
will not influence your decisions ; self-in-
terest will have no access to you. You
will rather seek him who has less desire to
make himself known, and all will bless your
justice and your indulgence, and will give
honour to God for whom you act.

"In all men you will see His image ; they
will find you unceasingly ready to be of
use to them. Feeling no rivalry with your
equals, — you will have pleasure in their

advantage; their successes will become
your own. Considering all as members of
one and the same family, destined to run
the same course, looking to the same end,
— the glory of the Chief, and the happiness
of all, will be ever the motives that incite
you. In this way, how will you not cause
our holy religion to be cherished. And
who knows if God, to encourage your
weak efforts and to reward your sacrifices,
will not make use of you to arrest some
souls on the point of abandoning Him, or,
to bring back others already fallen away.
Ah, my child, if He grant you this favour,
your entire life will not suffice to thank
Him. How admirable is He when He
uses such frail instruments to work His
mercies, and what happiness for him whom
He deigns to employ! . . . . Keep your
heart thus ready to do generously whatever
He may ask of you. But let us see now
what are the general and particular obstacles which you will have to combat.

" I do not pretend that religion does not demand sacrifices ; I know, and I have experienced only too well, that we are all born with a proneness to evil, which it is very difficult to overcome, and that before reaching that calm, that peace of which I have spoken to you, and which may be looked upon as a foretaste of heaven, one must have won many victories over himself. But I ask you, even if you were without religion, would you not experience the desire to rule the passions which might have power to master you? Would you not think, you who are constantly praising this human courage, whose consequences are sometimes so disastrous ; that there is grandeur of soul, nobleness, in making one's self master of all his movements, or at least in being able always to curb their effects? It seems to me that the greatest conqueror is nothing, when compared with the simple and virtuous man, whose whole study has been to know himself, and his glory, to rule

himself ; who, by the happy habit of repressing himself, has come to have nothing
ill-regulated ; who, always with calmness,
judges healthily of things, and chooses the
part which he deems the better, without being blinded by the impetuosity of his passions.

"The philosophers strove to make it
thought that they had reached this desir-
able condition. Religion gives me the
means of arriving there at the same time
that she proves to me the necessity of so
doing ; she does more ; she knows how to
make me love sacrifice, by showing it to
me on the road to heaven. Ah ! how much
more does a short meditation on the life
and passion of our Lord accomplish, than
all the arguments of cold reason, which tell
us, indeed, what is to be done, but do not
give us the strength to attain to it. It is
at the foot of your crucifix, my child, that
you will learn how to taste of real good ;
there you will appreciate that which the

world has to offer, and you will have no further pain in detaching yourself from it. These illusions vanish, and when the heart has once known truth, there is no other attraction for it. The cross will make you feel the heaviness of the iron chains which the world imposes, and the lightness of the gospel yoke. May the Lord give you grace to wear it always, and spare you the agonizing regret of having wavered between the world and Him. For I should never be able to bear the thought that you could fail to know Him, and thus make me sorry that I had given you birth. Know your Master, and you will have but one fear,— that of not doing enough for Him. After your falls, seek His goodness with the same confidence, which, in your early years, made you come and confess the faults of which I was sometimes ignorant ; through your ingenuousness, you found in my tenderness the consolation and the peace which you had lost. With what joy I pressed you then to my heart; often your tears made my own to flow, and I had enough to do in keeping them back. Well, my child, may this love, this indulgence, give you a feeble idea of the mercy, the tenderness of God's heart. If you have found these qualities in His weak, imperfect creature, how much more may you expect of Him from whom they proceed, who was the source of them, and the limits of whose love for you are only in His immensity. Remember again, that my cares, my tenderness for you seemed to increase in .proportion to your needs, or your infirmities ; and believe that your Heavenly Father experiences the same thing, but in the measure of a God. He is, then, a kind Physician who knows your wounds, who sounds the depth of them, who measures their extent, and sees their danger. He holds in His hand the remedies for your healing, and burns with the desire to apply them. One single turning only towards Him suffices, that His justice permit Him to satisfy His mercy, and then He pours that salutary balm which softens whatever of bitter the remedies may have held, and hastens their good result.

' "I confess, my child, that of all the sentiments I have experienced, that of maternity, a sentiment which takes away from none other, and yet surpasses all, has ever seemed to me most fitly to represent the love of God for His creatures. I constrain myself at times to think of Him as my judge, but I always find my Father again ! And however faithless I have been, however unworthy of being in the number of His children, I leave all to His love, and repeat to Him unceasingly : 'It is in Thee, Lord, and in Thee alone, that I have put my trust ; I cannot be confounded ; I have Thy word of promise.'

"May the heart of my dear child, then, filled with firm hope, attach itself to Him who alone can bring this hope to pass. This is a happiness of which it behooves not my ignorance, my weakness to speak, but of which a sensitive soul, detached from worldly interests, might have, I think, a faint idea. To love, and to love without limit, to love through all eternity the Object the most lovely, the most adorable, the source of every good, to have no longer cause to fear occasions of offending Him ; to see as God sees, to feel as He does, to be admitted to His divine intercourse, — what blessed happiness !

" Oh, my dear child ; if by my example, my faults, perhaps by my too great weakness towards you, I have given you any impression of religion other than the true one, it is at the feet of Jesus Christ that I ask your pardon for it; it is there that I pray Him that the punishments which my faults merit, may not fall on you. At His feet, too, I can attest that I have never made other wishes for you, than those which aimed at making you virtuous, and assuring to you the possession of this happiness.

"I call to my mind, my child, that, scarcely were you born, when I offered you to God ; and in the moment when I felt with transport the joy of being a mother, when my sufferings seemed to me too sweet since you were the price of them, when I would have found it just to pay with my life the happiness of giving birth to you, — ah, well, in that same moment I asked my God not to preserve you, except you were to love Him eternally. He received my sacrifice, and He has left you in existence ; is it not allowed me to hope that my prayer will be accomplished in all its greatness ?

"I conjure Thee, O God of goodness, have no regard to the weakness of her who prays to Thee, but consider that she intercedes for a child whom Thou hast given her in Thy mercy ; that this child is Thine, that I have never forgotten Thy right to her ; I have even feared that I might claim her as my own too much. Thou knowest that I never asked that she should have worldly goods nor any like thing ; but only this celestial dew whose preciousness I knew. Pour it upon her abundantly, my God. Thou only canst know how dear she is to me. . . . . Well, I accept whatever Thou hast in store for her, so that she be always faithful to Thee, and that after transmitting to her children the precious deposit of the faith in all its integrity, she may then love Thee and praise Thee for-ever."

These lines were written some months before the marriage. As the decisive hour approached, the wise mother specifies clearly what her heart had only sketched out.

"PARIS, *May* 15*th*, 1798.

"You ask me, my dear Ernestine, to give you a rule of conduct, an outline of the manner in which it will be well for you to mark out your time and dispose of it. I began by refusing you, convinced of my own incompetence, and thinking it better that

you should make this rule of life for yourself. Howbeit, touched by your confidence,
I am about to answer you, having first
asked for light from the Holy Spirit. This
practice of regulating the employment of
time, has been consecrated by the masters
of the spiritual life ; the Fénélons, the
Saint François de Sales, have always advised it for souls who would live Chris-
tianly, avoid offending God, and make some
progress in virtue. I doubt not that great
graces are connected with it. At the time
of my marriage, although still very young,
I felt this necessity, and reaped much fruit
from the rules planned by my fourteen
year's old head, and modified later by a
holy director. My knowledge of your character makes me add, my dear child, that
this practice is indispensable to you.

" The little aptitude you have for all that
comes under the head of pious practices,
your fear of everything that brings you
under subjection, the kind of prejudice you

have adopted, without much knowing why, against what you call *little observances*, — all this make it necessary for you to pre- scribe certain habits for yourself, with the resolution of being faithful to them. It is precisely because you dread everything that is small, that you must look at your motives supernaturally, and regard it as be- neath you to be guided only by your hu- mour or caprice.

" The rule of life, when it has been en- tered upon, will realize this aim, and will procure you the advantages of which I speak. All your actions will have the stamp of obedience, and that is the surest way of arriving, even when you don't sus- pect it, at the highest perfection. But I hasten to come to the details of the obliga- tions which this rule will impose upon you, for I see already your young courage is alarmed, and though your reason has asked this of me, yet your disposition fears it, tells you that it is good only for religious, and makes you dread the severity. It is important, then, to prove to you that Religion proportions herself to the weakness of our age, our health, even of our character ; that she asks of us only what is reasonable, and does but consecrate our duties.

"EMPLOYMENT OF THE DAY.

" 1st. You will stay eight hours in your bed : at your age this time for repose is necessary. The hour, then, when you go to bed, will determine your hour for getting up the next day ; but, except in case of unusual indisposition, or extraordinary fatigue, you will be exact in limiting yourself to the eight hours.

" 2d. Your first thought in waking will be for God ; you will offer your actions to Him, and invoke your good angel.

" 3d. As soon as you are dressed, you will say your prayer in the " Journée du Chrétien," or even a shorter one, if you know it ; but keep to the one which you adopt.

" 4th. You will read a chapter in the 'Imitation,' after which you will meditate for a quarter of an hour ; the two first books will suit you best for the present.

" 5th. You will hear mass every day.

" 6th. You will devote from an hour to an hour and a half to your breakfast, as well as to the duty you owe your grandparents.

" 7th. You will employ two hours in the morning, either in reading history, travels, or the like, or with masters in accomplishments ; if you wish to profit by your readings, you will make extracts.

" 8th. You will reserve a half hour for religious reading, and before beginning it, you will ask God for grace to get benefit from it.

" 9th. You will make your toilet before dinner, striving to spend no more time over it than is necessary. You might make use of these moments to learn some well-selected bits of poetry ; you would cultivate your memory, you would ornament your mind and prevent being too much taken up with fashion, so dangerous a thing for the young.

" 10th. I should like you to take up the habit of reflecting, five minutes only, before dinner, upon the way in which you have spent your morning and observed your rule.

" 11th. During the meal, while being as pleasant as possible out of consideration for your relatives, try to raise your heart to God from time to time. It would be well that the meal should not go over without some little practice of self-denial. For the present, confine yourself to repressing your too numerous fancies. Set about it gradually as yet, but you will find your health even will be the better for it.

" 12th. After dinner, stay with your relations for two hours; take up some needle-work at this time, and try to make it agreeable to others by the pleasantness of your society.

" 13th. You will then go to your room for two hours, or two hours and a half, during which you will say your beads some twenty times, and one penitential psalm, so that the seven psalms and the long rosary will be told in the week; the rest of the time will be given to reading, writing, or lessons in music or painting.

" 14th. The end of the evening will be devoted to your friends, to society, according to the tastes or the wish of your husband.

" 15th. You will keep the same rules for supper as for dinner. You will say your prayers in the evening, make your examination, and after asking God to forgive the faults of the day, and thanking Him for the blessings received, you will try to go to sleep with good thoughts of some kind.

" 16th. Your confessor alone can regulate the number of your communions; I should be glad, however, if you would make a resolution never to be kept away from the holy table, by your own fault, for more than a month, and if you wish to make confession easier, you will go to the confessional every fortnight.

"For three days before communion you will read daily a chapter of the 'Imitation,' the fourth book. You will keep a more careful watch over yourself ; you will discharge your duties with more exactness, knowing that it is chiefly the disposition of the heart that God asks of us.

"You will banish everything (except for a legitimate reason, the wish of your husband, for instance) that might distract you.

"You will continue the reading from the 'Imitation' for three days after, and will watch yourself with the same care, in giving thanks.

"It would be good to let some particular works of charity precede your approach to the sacraments.

"This rule, good for the time being, in that it is compatible with all your duties, might not suit you at another time; it could then be modified. It is quite enough, my dear child, that you promise not to change it without advice, but you would do well to accept, to propose, even, any change which seems reasonable to you, in view of a difference of circumstances. I am going to try, now, to write down for you some general rules, which, while fixing your mind on certain points, will make you avoid all anxiety.

" FIRST GENERAL RULE.

" As the first of all rules, the only one to which salvation is promised, is the doing one's duty, it is understood that the distribution of your time will always be subject to the wish, desire, and pleasure of your husband. Any time that his presence may interrupt one of your exercises, you will never look disturbed. You will leave off your prayers promptly, even when you may be finding them most comforting. At all times you will be animated by the desire of representing virtue to him as attractive, and to that end you will try to re-form the little defects of character that are still in you, and which would hinder this. When your exercises shall have been inter-rupted by your husband, or by something independent of your will, you will have no uneasiness about it, and, to avoid all confu-sion, you will take up your regular pursuits according to the time prescribed, at the moment when you are free again. You will take care, however to put the few prayers directed, and the religious reading, at the hour when you are used to be least inter-rupted.

" SECOND GENERAL RULE.

"To make your decision about anything that you may have to do, and which may not be comprised in this rule, you will ask if the action or the thing that you are going to undertake can be offered to God.

RULES FOR ALMS-GIVING.

" Every time that you receive your allowance you will take out the portion of the poor. You might fix it at a tenth of what you have at your disposal. I take it for granted that you would never have debts, for then you could n't give away, which would be the contradiction of justice.

" You will try to distribute your alms with discrimination, giving the preference to the old, the infirm, and those who are particularly consecrated to God.

" If you could sometimes, without omitting your duties, and always consulting the rules of prudence, if you could yourself see the sufferers, get them some comforts through your interest, cause them to bless religion and the God of charity, who has made use of you to help them, you would derive a very sweet satisfaction, and would only have to guard against following a perhaps too human inclination. I have no doubt that you would thus sometimes add to the sum set apart, what you had appropriated to a new fashion, or a superfluous article of dress, and this sacrifice would not be without its importance.

"RULES FOR YOUR READING.

" This subject is of interest to all ages, but especially to youth, when all impressions being more lively, a more or less judicious choice might have fatal results. I have no intention of speaking to you of books, either against religion or morals, or even of romances. Every Christian has renounced these at his baptism, and the principles that you now have satisfy me that you would have a horror of them ; but that is not enough ; resolve never to read religious books without advice. A book is good, useful at one time, which might be dangerous at another ; and he to whom God has trusted the care of your soul, has grace given him to decide for you.

"As to your books of instruction, or pleasure, it is sufficient that you determine not to choose them for yourself, and to consult only virtuous and wise persons."

Mademoiselle Ernestine is become Madame la Marquise de Rastignac ; the prudent mother had no wish to commit the future of her daughter to a brilliant but frivolous man, without principle, such as there were so many of at that time ; but she made choice of an upright man, serious, strongly attached to his duty, and whose religious feeling promised well for him.

Now, notwithstanding the recent and dreadful calamities, notwithstanding the atrocities which Paris has just witnessed, her society begins to whirl with festivities. One would say, in seeing the eagerness of this great world, still dyed with the blood of its martyrs, that it would fain make up for its sacrifices by dizzying itself in the vortex of pleasures.

The seventeen years old marchioness is one of the most invited, and most fêted ; her literary advantages, her lively and sparkling wit, her sportive disposition, attract admiration and praises which hide a twofold snare. At this age intoxication is easy ; one yields himself willingly to the happiness of feeling himself loved, or sought, ... the good and confiding nature of the young woman has no suspicion of the malignity of a world as envious as flattering, but her honest conscience hears the reproach within, "God is not satisfied — He asks something different." A filial outpouring consoles this soul made for virtue ; she confides to her mother what many a one will not own to himself. She is encouraged to find a stay as tender as it is strong, and quite happy to take refuge in holiness and love at the same time.

Under the impression of a sweet joy, and of a real alarm, the mother responds by new counsels, to which she adds the most urgent solicitation.

"MONTMIRAIL, *December* 28, 1799.

" The last talks with you filled me with comfort, my dear Ernestine ; it is true, the more satisfaction I had in them, the more is your departure made painful to me. Thus, I like to tell you that they left a tender impression with me, in which my soul loves to rest. The light which God in His mercy gives you about yourself,— an inestimable favour, which often one does not possess until he is much older, — the fulness of your confidence, and more than that, the teachableness of your mind ; this is what fills me with hope. Yes, I rejoice, my dear child, but a mother's heart passes very quickly from hope to fear, and I feel the need to speak for a few moments with you of the different reasons which make me go from the one to the other. May heaven make my advice useful to you. May my tenderness justify in your eyes the alarm which is perhaps premature, but, I believe, well founded.

"You complain of a weakness in your character which gives you the appearance of agreeing with the person who is talking with you, and which prevents your resisting everything that is not absolutely bad in itself; you feel in yourself the desire to please, a coquetry of mind which makes you seek by preference those whom you consider superior, because their approbation is more flattering to you. You are disposed towards general benevolence, which might well be a virtue, and proceed from the goodness of your heart, but that it has also for motive this immoderate desire that you have for approbation. The outcome is, that regard for human opinion has daily an increased empire over you, and the weakness by which you allow yourself to be misled prevents you from freeing yourself from it. Your delicate conscience warns you about the least things, but the fear of being blamed and thought a poor-spirited person renders you

deaf to its voice. This combat grows painful to you, and then you seek to persuade
yourself that the question is not of the
first necessity ; you say to yourself, that in
religion one may put aside what is only
advised, in order to make a point only of
what is binding ; that in youth there would
be inconveniences in adopting a line of
conduct which one could not be sure of
following. You put off for a more advanced age practices of which you feel the
necessity, but which a few light words
cause you to neglect. You set apart God's
part; you limit it, and you let the world
take its portion and increase it in proportion as the other diminishes. This division,
however, does not procure you the tranquillity which you seek, for the mercy of
your God pursues you ; you cannot enter
into yourself without blushing for your
weakness, without being humiliated even
(you have confessed as much yourself), for
the claim that this weakness has estab-

lished upon you, and without being frightened at the abyss into which it may plunge
you. . . . . 'But I do no harm,' do you
say? Is it not a wrong, then, to refuse to
God what one feels that He asks ; to cheat
one's self of the graces that attach to
fidelity ; to expose himself to lose those
which he has, by resistance ; and lastly,
supposing that you do no evil, you do not
all the good which you ought, and to which
you are destined. The more God gives
you a horror for vice, and inclination for
virtue, the more He urges its practice in
your soul ; the greater are your pledges to
Him, the more guilty you are if you cease
to fulfil them. Do you think, dear Ernestine, that this energy, this highness of sentiment, this strength amid so great weakness which would make you capable of great
sacrifices, this gentleness, this evenness of
temper, this kindness, this gratitude, which
you express in such a touching way, do you
think that they should be limited to be mere

moral qualities, and that He who has put in your heart the precious germ of so many virtues, has not a right to exact that they shall be exercised for Him, and can you be at peace so long as you prevent their use and prevent them from rising to the source from whence they proceed? But let not your sensibility be terrified, for these same qualities will be only the more endearing and lovable when they shall have been so directed.

"In the picture that I have just drawn, my child, it seems to me that you cannot fail to recognize yourself; for it is the faithful portraiture of all that the frankness of your confidence has revealed to me, and it is on this confession that I base my hopes; when an evil is acknowledged, it is very near being cured. There needs, then, only a strong, persevering will to bring about the remedy, and you will ask this of Him whom you pray so earnestly not to abandon you.

"I must tell you, joyfully, that in writing I feel all my fears vanish ; my mission to you is full of consolation. If I had to open your eyes to yourself, to combat your illusions, I could be uneasy, because of the feebleness of my parts ; but here the mercy of God has done all. I speak to a soul which knows its own misery, which bewails the gulf towards which that misery is drawing it, whilst a powerful hand holds it back, to which, doubtless, it will not fail to surrender itself. If I had to undeceive you about the enchanting fascination of all earthly things, your great youth and the perils to which you are exposed might alarm me ; but happy, happy mother, I have only to congratulate myself ; scarcely have you tasted these delights when you feel their hollowness and insufficiency. Your heart finds nothing here that can satisfy it. You examine men, — you have already passed judgment upon them ; you say that they are nearly all foolish, and that the number of the wise is very small; how is it to be thought, then, that you could sacrifice your conscience, your peace of mind, your eternal happiness, to acquire the esteem of people whom you scorn, and of a world whose corruption horrifies you? And why, setting aside the powerful reasons which I doubt not will determine you, should you not prefer the approval of that small number, which assuredly you admit to have chosen the better part, since you style them wise? Besides, would it not be easy to prove to you that they who have done most to merit a vain esteem have never won it?

"The world, inconsistent in its conduct, is not always so in its judgments, and do you know who are the people towards whom its railleries and sarcasms are most surely directed? It is those weak characters, those narrow minds which, belonging neither to God nor the world, go on floating in their uncertainty, not doing the good they love, nor avoiding the evil that they fear. They lay themselves open to ridicule by their inconsistencies, and reap, as the fruit of their pains, only the general scorn due to the cowardice of their behaviour. Therefore, humanly speaking, what is necessary to get men's esteem? To be in harmony with one's self, to be virtuous, and believe that this worldling who vents his malignity in mocking, if he finds you beyond attack, does homage in his soul to the principles against which he inveighs only because they are his condemnation. Your personal interest, then, is found to be at one with religion; it teaches you to despise men's judgments, while you see that this is the surest way to get their esteem. Religion asks no more, but she is not content with so stingy a reward. What encouragements does she not offer! What hopes! What arguments of every kind! Ah, my child, lift yourself for a moment above all that is created; behold the heavenly treasures, and then, if it be possible, be ambitious for the earthly ! See the crown which awaits you, which is promised to your courage, to your perseverance, and then estimate the frivolities, the toys with which men amuse themselves here below. Fill yourself with love of your God, and you will quickly know how to value the esteem and the friendship of men. Go into your own heart, and you will find Him there. He calls you, He entreats you, He awaits you, and gives to you a feeling of unchangeable peace whenever you have recourse to Him, and submit yourself to his divine will. You will try in vain to find peace elsewhere.

"What, then, holds you back, my dear Ernestine ? Your mind is convinced, yea, more, it is enlightened ; your heart is touched ; you blush for your weakness ; should you still yield to it ? What have you to put in the balance ? The jests of those who will not have the strength to imitate you, ... the railing of a few godless ones, ... no, such puerile fear will not make you hesitate henceforward ; you will not set yourself up as a preacher; this rôle has not devolved upon you, and in sooth you would not have acquired this right ; but a firm behaviour and constant, in harmony with your principles, this will be your mission ; you will join with it, according to your possibility, all the attraction that gayety, amiability, and simplicity can offer, to make it more efficacious. The gentle, quiet, and reserved manner in which you will receive all the bad jokes launched against you will soon take away all desire to make them. You will give no handle against you, because all will be regulated and consistent. This conduct, sustained for two or three years only, will gain for you complete liberty ; the world will weary of persecuting you. Certain of being able to gain nothing, it will exercise its mischievousness upon others, whom your example will, perhaps, help to sustain. You will be greatly astonished, at the end of a few years of oblivion, to see those same persons who may have seemed to treat you as a mean-spirited and narrow person, seek you out, consult you in puzzling situations, prop themselves by the reputation you have acquired, and feel honoured by any interest which you may take in them. . . . . But, my child, why fall back upon human . motives, which I am quite willing should encourage and sustain you for the moment, but which are not made for a soul like yours. If you needed similar incentives, could I forget that your attitude towards me, your confidence, your sentiments, give me the most powerful that I could offer you, and that to speak to you of my happiness, my satisfaction, would be to decide you? But, far be it from me to stop you there; your heart, moreover, speaks to you, mine feels it only too deeply. . . . . No, my child, we will both have purer and more powerful motives, and the mother of

Ernestine will show herself worthy of her confidence, by teaching her to know the only real good, the only interest for which one should sacrifice everything. Run the race that is open to you, but never lose from sight the eternity which ends it; let all your actions which tend toward this goal be hallowed and animated by this hope. Ah, my child, *there* is the happiness which my heart solicits for you, that for which I would lay down my life, my repose ; it is there that I desire to possess you, and to find you again, no more to leave you."

This language was understood by the lovely young woman, so truly worthy of her mother, in spite of the sensible difference of their characters. There was the same elevation and generosity of sentiment. The Lord had placed them side by side ; one to call out abundantly the treasures of wisdom contained in the maternal heart ; the other to bring a counterpoise to all the

seductions of mind and heart, for, notwithstanding a precocious maturity, notwithstanding the light of faith which illumi-
nates certain souls at a tender age, and
makes them say with the wise man, even
before having made the experiment, "Vanity of vanities, all is vanity, except to love
God and to serve Him;" it is rare that
youth is exempt from sweet illusions, and
gracious and very natural hopes which may
perfectly agree with the purest longings
and the holiest affections.

Soon a new happiness and new duties
came to fill this new existence, where life
seemed to run over.

Madame de Rastignac received her little
Zénaïde with transports of love, and she re-
solved to bring her up, as she had been
herself brought up by the most watchful
and devoted of mothers. To complete her
joy, she heard at the same time, that her
father was hastening towards France. For,
in fact, Monsieur de Doudeauville, impa-

tient to see his family, had set forth on the
first news of the fall of the Directory (18th
Brumaire, '99), without waiting for the decree of armistice expected from the first
consul by all the emigrants ; but the difficulties of the journey this time were encountered in the foreign countries, which,
defeated by Bonaparte, now distrusted all
the French. By the aid of his title of
Spanish grandee, under the name of Ambrosio, born a quarter of an hour's distance
from Madrid (the Castle of Madrid in the
Bois de Bologne being only half a league
from Paris), the Duke of Doudeauville,
without telling falsehoods, traversed Austria and Italy as a Spaniard. He got as
far as Lyons, from whence he intended to
proceed the next day, when a letter from
his wife stopped him : being anxious, she
begs him to wait for regular papers before
finishing his journey. He submits, not
without a struggle, for when one has nearly
reached a long desired goal, minutes be-

come hours.   After eight days of unbear
able waiting, receiving nothing, he decides
to take up his journey, and, with the perversity one often sees in the affairs of this
poor world, hardly has he left Lyons when
the good duchess reaches it ; to make the
greatest speed, she has travelled night and
day.   Arrived at the hotel, she eagerly
asks for Monsieur Ambrosio.

"; Madame will surely breakfast."

"Dear me, no ; I only want Monsieur
Ambrosio !"   Seeing the surprise of the
landlady, Madame de Doudeauville adds instantly, "this gentleman is my husband."

To satisfy her impatience, they turn over
the leaves of the strangers' book, and tell
her that after staying for ten days in Lyons, Monsieur Ambrosio has just left. . . . .
Much annoyed, and not understanding this
conduct, which a lost letter explained, the
noble traveller exclaims : "How strange it
is, ... and what could he do here ?"
The landlady, misunderstanding the feel-

ing which agitates her, thinks it her duty to say : " Be reassured, madam, he led a perfectly correct life here. He went to walk a great deal, but alone with his little dog." In spite of her disappointment, Madame de Doudeauville cannot help laughing, and answers that she is not uneasy on that score. Then she asks for post-horses, and hastens her departure.

The meeting takes place at Mâcon. Ignoring her fatigue and poor health, in order not to delay the happiness of them all, the happy duchess wishes to continue her journey : very soon the whole family is reunited.

Holy Scripture says of the virtuous woman : " The heart of her husband doth safely trust in her, so that he shall have no need of spoil. She considereth a field and buyeth it. Her children rise up and call her blessed ; her husband also, and he praises her." The application is easy ; not only had Madame de Doudeauville preserved by her courage all her property, but, says the duke, " She had beautified it by her cares, and improved it by a wise administration.

" The first time that she conducted me to one of our estates, she presented it to me like a conquest, with a sweet and modest pride, which became her well. I, who had for long despaired of seeing myself in these mourned-for places ; I whose ambition in my days of exile had been to be able to retain my gardener's house thus, I thought I dreamed in finding myself reinstated as master.

" The benevolent fairy to whom I owed the preservation of this beautiful domain had paid me the delicate attention of appointing as steward my valet de chambre, whom I had sent back to France eight years before.

" This excellent man, who had been with me from my tenderest childhood, embraced me with transport, while he wept

with emotion. His tears called forth my
. own.

"This was only the prelude to what I
was to experience in Paris, on finding again
my mother, my children, some relatives,
and devoted friends. It was a joy, a whirl,
an intoxication!"

Alas! a few pages farther on we read:
"The happiness which I tasted with my
own dear ones, was not to be of long
duration."

CHAPTER VI.

DEATH OF MADAME DE RASTIGNAC.

Up to this time, as we have seen, suffering has not been lacking to the precious existence whose course we love to follow; as the charming young child, the gracious young woman, the brilliant court lady — in whatever situation we consider her, we see always those shades of earth, which an ignorant hand would wish to banish, but without which we have beneath our eyes only the flat representation of fleeting enjoyment.

For the Duchess of Doudeauville, these shadows, these trials, were always growing heavier; during the torture of the Revolution, she trembled for the beings most dear to her; she felt every fear, every apprehension; only the Lord was almost contented that she should *foresee* and *accept* the greatest sacrifices. A visible angel to all her own, she was marvellously guarded and defended in her turn by a celestial protector. But at last the sword must pierce through her soul, and like the Virgin of Sorrows, towards whom she feels drawn, she finds her appointed place at the foot of the cross ; we shall see her there, brave and generous, bow to the hand of God. She has braved the scaffold, but she is to have her martyrdom still, one which all mothers will understand.

In the very midst of festivities, and in the intoxication of the tenderest joys, Madame de Rastignac suddenly feels a serious failing of health ; a persistent cough, accompanied by fever, a general condition of weakness, sad symptoms of a grave disease, — these cause alarm in a family whose delight she is ; for, if she gave to the world her gayety and the graces of her mind, she reserved her whole heart for her own people.

Relying on the good air of Montmirail as the best remedy, her mother takes her there in the course of July, 1802 ; but instead of being checked, the malady becomes more evident, and, towards the end of August, they hasten back to Paris, where they can find all the resources of art. Madame de Doudeauville then installs herself in her daughter's room ; for nearly three months she passes her days there, and often her nights too, hanging upon the beating of her heart, watching in her face the progress of an illness of whose gravity she has a pre-sentiment, while with all her might she clings to the faintest ray of hope. But the Lord does not permit a long truce to those whom He has chosen to glorify Him more especially. To the sacrifices which each day exacts, He adds harder trials ; He makes them drink, at times, of the deep waters of tribulation ; and that which is an alarm to the erring or slumbering soul is a recompense to the faithful soul, become the spouse, the friend ; to whom the Lord says, as once to his favoured disciples : " Can ye drink of my cup ? "

Let us follow the mother and daughter in this last struggle, where they rival each other in faith, self-abnegation, and generosity. A letter of Monsieur l'Abbé Legris-Duval has left us a document upon these last hours, precious for its touching edification. Profoundly anxious, but always mistress of herself, Madame de Doudeauville, so soon as she perceives the danger, desires that the minister of the Lord should come to aid, sustain, console, and if it needs must be, to prepare for her departure the child of her love. What she proposes is very simple ; the priest has always had his place at the fireside ; he is a family friend, and as such he comes to talk with the invalid, to speak to her of the many graces attached to suffering, of the merits which she may acquire. These strengthening words are welcomed by a soul accustomed from its infancy to read in the great book of the Divine Will.

"In loving my mother," says Madame de Rastignac, "I learned to love virtue. I always thought it the voice of God that I heard when she spoke, and in obeying her, I felt it to be His will that I did."

The beginnings of the disease were marked by the terror due to vague and sad presentiments ; then she invoked God, and afterwards, turning towards her mother, she said to her : "Stay with me ; near you I have never been afraid of anything." And she slept tranquilly in this safe-keeping.

The hope of entire and quick recovery came quickly to this ardent nature prone to confidence, then the fears returned. She hid them carefully from her mother, her father, her husband ; but at times she allowed others to see her forebodings. Feeling herself more ill, she said one day : —

"I am resigned to all God may will, but I confess that it would cost me much to give up life."

" That is natural," said some one, " at twenty-one years, with all the advantages that insure happiness."

" No," she said, laughing, " these are no ties ; you don't understand me."

" But you are a wife and a mother ! "

" Ah, I feel that more keenly than ever ! And I am a daughter." These last words, pronounced in an accent of tenderness and grief, were heart-rending.

She who in infancy had found her happiness in relieving the poor, whose greatest pleasure had been to give, provided that her charities were kept secret, she who had always been kind and devoted to her parents, friends, and servants, forgot herself up to the last moment, in busying herself with thought for others. Six weeks before her death, a prey to the sharpest sufferings, she had set her mind upon writing to her husband who was kept away from her in spite of himself. She feared that the sight of a strange handwriting might cause him uneasiness.

Her condition now forbidding her to keep long any one position or to make any movement without acute pain, the desire of practising patience, and the fear of afflicting those about her, arrested every complaint, stifled every sigh, and when, surprised by the violence of the suffering, she let a groan escape her, she would temper the impression thus made by a smile, a reassuring word. Each one received tokens of her goodness; her servants rendered her no service that she did n't show her satisfaction. To distract her father from his alarm, she would cast about her for anything that might interest him. As soon as her husband returned, they had good talks together. They spoke of the future, and especially of a plan made for mutual sanctification.

Every day the invalid begged her mother to read a chapter from the Gospel to her, on which she made comments; and after the reading she would kiss the holy book respectfully. "At what are you astonished," she said to those who saw her, "is it not the word of God?"

On the 30th of October, thinking her not ill enough to receive the Holy Viaticum, Monsieur Lévis brought her the communion at midnight. The next day, the joy and sensible improvement of the sick woman attested her happiness.

"How good the Lord is," she said, "can one ever love Him enough? How He repays us for our sacrifices! Could I refuse Him one? .... We make so many for the world! Let Him dispose of me as He will, I am sure that it will always be for my good."

She even came to cherish her sufferings. "I should be sorry to have less pain," she often said; "Jesus Christ bore much greater suffering." She made it a rule to accept what was offered to her, in spite of any repugnance, in memory of the vinegar and myrrh given to her Saviour.

In the early days of November a new consultation pronounced the disease incurable. Her father was present. The mother, at the daughter's side, awaited the answer, in mortal apprehension ; they took care not to bring it to her. But the silence revealed everything. .Without asking any questions, as soon as the doctors are gone, she hastens to the foot of the altar, her ordinary refuge ; here she meets her husband, and reads in his tear-stained eyes the terrible decree, offers with him her sacrifice, calls the Virgin of Sorrows to her aid, and returns to her daughter with a face of perfect calmness. In respect to her silence, the invalid, who knows that her fate has been decided, asks no question, and when they try to sound her thoughts, she is content to answer, " I am in the hands of Providence, as it were in my mother's arms."

However, in spite of the forebodings intensified at intervals, Madame de Rastignac, as is often the case in this disease, hoped for a cure. God allows these alternations to give the dying person the merit of the sacrifice, and yet not to have him always facing a weight too crushing for his weakness. Being warned by her confessor, Monsieur Lévis, she seemed astonished to be so near her end, but, as always, her thought was for her mother. She feared that this presage of the last sacraments might give her a mortal blow; and, lest another should wound this heart whose tenderness she knew, she would give to no one the charge of preparing her.

This woman of twenty, before whom the tomb is opening, and who can hardly speak, is about then to encourage her mother to see her die. Calling her to her bedside, as soon as the confessor is gone, she says to her, " Monsieur Lévis has proposed to me to receive the sacraments in a day or two ; do you not think it would be for my

13

edification? Extreme Unction never does harm."

With her soul torn within her, but calm and tranquil in appearance, the mother says in answer everything that religion and tenderness can inspire at such a moment. The sick woman being reassured, then allows her heart to speak freely: "I did not think myself so ill; the veil has just been torn away; I must die; this news having moved me, I had need of you to set myself right."

Let us hear the answer, worthy of the mother of the Maccabees: "My daughter, if God sees in your heart the submission of Isaac, and in mine the faith of Abraham, perhaps He will turn aside the sword! . . . . But let us call to our mind Jesus Christ, His obedience, His self-devotion."

"O my mother; my only friend, you know why I should regret life; . . . . but fear nothing, your daughter will be worthy of you."

She was indeed so, for a little after she added in a steady voice: " Before you go out of the room, the sacrifice must be made with the perfection that God demands. . . . . Mother, my sacrifice is accomplished. . . . . Let us bless God, calmness is restored. But if any trace of emotion be visible, they might be afflicted. Let us read a chapter in the 'Imitation.'" They opened at hazard, and fell upon this chapter: " On the royal road of the holy cross." The mother emphasizes these words, " In the cross is the strength of soul ; in the cross, the joy of the mind, the consummation of virtue, the perfection of holiness. If you bear the cross with a good heart, it will carry you on and conduct you to the longed-for goal, where you will cease to suffer."

"Take up your cross, then, and follow Jesus, and you will attain ·to eternal life."

The invalid, encouraged, enraptured, cries with transport: " What a treasure is the cross ! . . . . It is very true, that death is a gain, and suffering an actual good."

Remembering, then, some trifling details of which she had spoken to her mother, she imparts them to her, and adds: "I thank God in dying, that I have never had a single thought which was unknown to you."

Leaving her daughter peaceful and full of confidence, the poor mother, broken by the effort which she had just made, retires for a moment. Pale, with choking breath, she was heard to say, from time to time, without shedding a tear : "I hope no longer ; my daughter is going to die."

Aware of her danger, the sick woman wished to know the exact degree. On the next day she asked to speak alone with the physician. The conversation was a kind of interrogatory, and in questioning the doctor most eagerly, she watched his eyes, his expression, his smallest movement. The answer was a sentence which his humanity wished in vain to mitigate. She heard it, without being troubled, and without moving, ... while the physician, his heart heavy, his mind struck by so great youth, trouble, and courage united, declared that he could not recover from the impression during the entire day.

The moments grew precious ; the sick woman spoke to the Abbé Legris-Duval, on that very day, of the blessedness of receiving the sacraments.

" It will be to-morrow," she added.

" To-morrow ? Your mother, your husband know about it; they would surely wish that this sad duty were discharged as soon as possible. The waiting will be cruel to these loving hearts.""

" You are right ; I do not wish to make them suffer; I shall cost them sorrow enough. It shall be this evening. I wish to spare the feelings of my relatives this scene, but I have begged my mother to be here ; it would be too hard for her to keep away. Besides, I need her presence; she is my good angel; she is my life; I could indeed believe I have never done anything well without her; I owe to her cares the prolonging of my days, and to her virtues my salvation."

At the news of the ceremony which was to take place, the whole household seemed to have been struck by a sentence of death. The old servants wept as if they were going to lose one of their own children; consternation is spread abroad; but by the sick-bed peace reigns. Fear and anxiety seem banished from this sanctuary, where the constancy of the mother and the resignation of the daughter have triumphed. How grand they are, both of them, in these last moments. The mother, on her knees, controls her tears, and allows only accents of faith to escape from her heart, uniting her prayers with those of the church; offering the hands of the daughter herself for the Extreme Unction. She, peaceful and perfectly collected, responds to the prayers with a steady voice.

"This is the body of your Saviour," says the priest to her; "do you believe this?"

"Ah! how I believe it!" she cries; and these words were emphasized with such fervour of love, that those who heard wept in repeating them.

After the ceremony the fever abated, the rest of the day was calm, her powers seemed to take on more life, but the next day the condition became so alarming, that more than once they thought the last moment had come. With her eyes fixed upon the crucifix, the sick woman repeated lovingly: "I unite my sufferings to Thine, my Saviour. Thy merits are infinite; they will supply my insufficiency."

Towards evening she asked for the Abbé Legris-Duval. "Be my interpreter to my mother when I shall be no more," she said to him. "Conjure her to live after I am gone, in spite of her sorrow; express to her this, my last wish."

" You feel very ill, then ? "

" Yes, very ill."

" The poor mother ! .... But you will pray God to comfort her ? "

"Oh, yes ; but soothe you her grief ; persuade her to take care of herself."

" Your mother has ties and duties left which are dear to her ; she will attend to her health, you may be sure ; but at all events, if we must ask it of her, who can do it better than you ? Speak to her yourself ; we shall be sure of being heard, if we recall to her what her dying daughter has said."

" This very evening, I will get her promise to live and act as mother towards my little girl. I hope that she will find Ernestine again in Zénäide. Monsieur de Rastignac has already begged her to adopt the child, and she has consented. How happy is my daughter ; she will be brought up by my mother."

There was more conversation ; she added in conclusion : " What will you do for me when I am dead ? "

" I shall mourn for you, as all will do who know you, and I shall pray God for you."

" And I ? — I shall be busy for you all in heaven."

" You are sure of going there, then ? "

" I have that confidence. I abandon myself entirely to God, and I am without solicitude."

A sinking condition followed. Madame de Doudeauville came in haste, and being alone with her mother, the sufferer, with a touching confidence, implores her to keep up for the sake of all her dear ones. She bequeaths to her her dear Zénaïde. She then begs that they will ask the Abbé Legris-Duval to come back again, as she desires to dictate her last wishes to him.

" Never," says he, " had I seen her more herself, or more lovely, and yet she was in a kind of agony. Cold sweats, continual sinkings, hiccoughings, announced the supreme moment." She asked him to take her writing-desk, and added : —

"I wish to make my will, for, I am of age; I am twenty-one years old."

"A will, madame? I am not a notary; I do not know the proper form."

"It is only some provision for my parents, and for Monsieur de Rastignac; I have never had anything to do but to make my desires known to them; besides, I will sign, ... if I can, for I am very weak. I would like to say that I leave the world with resignation, but grieving deeply for my family, — arrange all that."

The dying woman, recalling then all the memories, all the affections of her life, expressed herself with so much ardour, that her secretary could hardly follow her. "How many tears I shall cause my mother! And what a sacrifice to leave her! She has always made me so happy! People have said that my education was too severe. How little they knew my mother. . . . . If I had to complain, it would be of too much happiness; perhaps I was too much accustomed to fulfil my duties, through sentiment for her. She has known how to make everything agreeable to me, through my one idea of pleasing her. It is the truth ; you have witnessed this yourself. . . . . Promise me to repeat to her often, that she made the happiness of her daughter, and if I have caused her pain, implore her to pardon me."

Afterwards she spoke of her father ; she compassionated his misfortunes : " So young to have been banished from his people for ten years, and to come back to his family only to see his daughter die before his eyes! It will make him very unhappy ! My brother Sosthènes will take my place to him; he will do better than I. Tell him that I counted on his good heart, and that this idea comforted me in dying. Tell Monsieur de Rastignac that I wished to live to make him happy." Then she spoke of her aunt, Madame de Montesquiou, whom she loved very much, because she had always told her the truth.

At the end, she wished to sign, but the good duchess had to be called, to place the writing-desk comfortably. Her daughter hastened to prepare her. "Mother," she said, laughing, "I am very weak; that must be the case when one makes his will; my hand trembles; I think I am losing my memory, too. How must I write la Rochefoucauld?" And she continued to laugh.

Sustaining her daughter with one hand, and steadying the paper with the other, the courageous mother peacefully dictated each letter of the signature.

This last night was cruel; all the house were up. The sick woman seeing a servant come into her room, said to him: "Why don't you go to bed? I would rather not disturb anybody."

At the moment when her mother is her only support, she entreats her to go and take some rest; on her refusing, she insists. Then the poor mother goes, but only to hide herself in the corner of the room.

She stays there for two whole hours, not daring to move, scarcely breathing, for fear of being perceived. At last, she allows herself to be torn away, as her daughter seems better ; but a moment or two after, she comes in again. "Mother," says the dying one, "the hour is come. Shall we both have courage ? "

The Abbé Legris-Duval, coming in at that moment, stands dumb with admiration before the picture presented to him. The expiring one has already put on the celestial glory of a transported serenity. Her mother stands at her side, her eyes riveted on her daughter. She is calm, but affecting in her intense expression of maternal anguish. She is great in all the majesty of religion and misfortune. Addressing herself to the priest, the young woman says :

" I am about to die ; will you promise not to leave me until the end ? "

" Ah, madame, I should have asked that of you as a favour."

" Nor you, either, my good mother ? " A gentle embrace assures her. She adds : "Let us make an act of renunciation as perfect as possible. My God, I surrender into Thy hands my soul and my life. I abandon all my interests to Thy love ; do with me as it pleases Thee. I unite my sufferings and my death to that of Jesus Christ, in whom alone I hope."

Having thus expressed her own feeling, she asks them to pray with her, and repeats the acts of love and of faith pronounced by the priest, as if already she felt herself in the sensible presence of her God. While the witnesses of these last moments withdrew to give free course to their tears, the mother, always completely self-controlled, stays by her daughter, joins in her act of sacrifice, and makes her repeat it.

All the house being assembled for the prayers of those in extremity, the sick woman turns to her father, and collecting all her strength, asks aloud for a last blessing.

He springs towards his daughter, embraces and blesses her. " Father, spare me," she says to him ; " I feel too much the sacrifices I have to make."

Her mother, on her knees, betrays herself this time ; her tears flow. " Preserve your courage," says Ernestine to her ; " we shall need it to the end." The husband, the brother, also, have their turn, and receive the last farewell which is only a rendezvous for heaven. Hope was so vivid, that it already transported the dying one to the happy term of exile. " Shall I be in heaven soon ? Is life about to end ? When shall I see my God ?" Then moderating her desire, she added : " Let us not yield ourselves to impatience ; that would be giving place to temptation." She confided to the minister of Jesus Christ, with simplicity, her slightest imperfections, and when she could no longer make herself quite heard, her mother interpreted her confession.

In the morning, when the Holy Sacrifice

is offered with her intention, she renews
her own sacrifice, her sufferings being extreme. "I am making my purgatory," she
says, joyfully, as she keeps her eyes fixed
upon the crucifix, and upon an image of the
Blessed Virgin, which she kisses in turn,
pronouncing the name of Jesus and Mary.
Her last words were for her God and for
her who had taught her to love Him. Feeling her tongue stiffen, she turns and says
in a dying voice : " Mother, forgive me and
bless your daughter."

Although she had received the holy Viaticum three days before, Monsieur Lévis,
thinking that so great faith and generosity
authorized a dispensation, proposes to ad-
minister the Holy Communion again. "It
is all that I desire," she says, with transport. They make haste ; the time is short.
For a moment her eyelids drop ; she seems
to lose the use of her senses ; but scarcely
is she in the presence of Him who has
said "I am the resurrection and the life,"

when her eyes open, and she is conscious of her privilege. She had feared that she might not be able to swallow the wafer, but with an impulse full of simple frankness, she cries : "Mother, I was able to receive it." These were her last words. At the same moment she lost consciousness, but without agitation or effort. Her condition was more like the peace of a soul lost in sweet contemplation, than the last failing of nature.

While those who stood by, bathed in tears, asked each other whether she was in heaven or on earth, the dying woman bends her head towards her mother, and gives up her soul so gently, that Monsieur Lévis is the first to perceive it.

But the pious duchess, on her knees, motionless, watches still for a movement, a breath. She calls Ernestine ; no one dares to answer. At last, Monsieur Lévis, without saying a word, draws the crucifix from the daughter's hands, and places it in those

14

of the mother. How touching, how sublime was this afflicted mother. . . . . Not a
murmur, not a cry, but a torrent of tears,
hitherto restrained, now suddenly deluges
this cross. She seizes it, embraces it, and
pressing it to her lips, seems to wish that
she too might leave her last sigh there.

A moment after she rises, approaches
her daughter, puts her mouth a hundred
times to the half open mouth, the lifeless
eyes, questions her with her gaze, embraces
her again, and sits down to see her better,
and to satisfy her hunger for the last time
with this heart-rending spectacle.

After a moment of silence, Monsieur de
Doudeauville proposes to his wife to withdraw. "I will do what you like," she answers, "though I am better off here than
anywhere else." A few more minutes having gone by, he insists anew, and entreats
her to go away. She gets up then, goes
towards the bed, falls on her knees, makes
a short prayer, again embraces those dear

remains, and without a gesture or a cry, leaves her daughter forever.

Having gone down to her family, she receives them with touching sweetness. But the measure of her strength is spent. Soon she loses consciousness and falls into a sort of delirium, succeeded by profound exhaustion ; and yet in the intensest moment of her grief she keeps the expression and the feeling of complete resignation.

CHAPTER VII.

PRIVATE LIFE.

JUST as one cannot prevent at times a feeling of sadness in seeing the season decline, so, when arrived at the middle of its course, cold often enters the poor human heart, which measures by its own experience the value of all good here below. But let us not pity the heart, for at this moment a rich and abundant harvest is preparing; if the autumn has not the charms and perfumes of the fresh season, it has others no less agreeable, and more precious for their usefulness.

Howbeit the second part of the existence of Madame de Doudeauville exhibits less brilliant features, it is not less rich in miracles of grace and holiness. Her mission continues; the past has given her an irresistible empire over her own people ; in her constant labour to keep herself in the background, whilst devoting herself to the happiness of all about her, she has become sovereign of the hearts which willingly suffer an ascendency exercised with so great love and modesty! The sight of her recalls the canticle of her who is her model, — "My soul doth magnify the Lord, ... He hath regarded the lowliness of his handmaiden!" In truth, while a thanksgiving is always on her lips, even after the greatest sacrifices, it seems as if the breath of vanity had no power to touch her. The blow just fallen has left in her heart a profound impression of sadness ; the image of her daughter, ever before her eyes, brings her yet oftener to the foot of the cross ; it is not distraction that is wanted by this truly afflicted mother ; she has need to unite her sorrow with that of Calvary.

One of the dominant thoughts of the

virtuous duchess since the Revolution has
been to contribute with all her power to
set up the overturned altars, to restore the
pious monuments to their proper destina-
tion, and the parishes to their legitimate
pastors. As soon as calm was somewhat
established, on going to live on her favourite estate, whose name she had borne
before her marriage, she hastened to take
the necessary steps with the authorities,
sparing neither trouble nor sacrifice of all
kinds, to put a faithful priest in the place
of the intruder who was supplying the
church of Montmirail. Thanks to her
care, and, above all, to her liberality, the
new curé also entered the vicarage, which
had been transformed for several years
into barracks.

Whilst she was herself negotiating all
these affairs, and before they had arrived
at a happy conclusion, she bought at Montléan, a suburb of Montmirail, the remains
of an old Benedictine priory. She desired

in this way to save the church from total destruction, to have a sure place where the Catholic worship would be exercised, and to make an honourable amend to the Lord for the outrages committed during the Revolution. Another reason which determined her to buy this priory, was the pitiable state in which she found the asylum founded by the lamented John de Montmirail ; the sick poor were in uncomfortable premises, given into hired hands, without any true comfort for soul or body. Madame de Doudeauville formed the project of appropriating the greater part of the buildings of Montléan to this hospital.

In the time of the Gondi de Retz, the Castle of Montmirail had sheltered Saint Vincent de Paul, then tutor to the famous cardinal ; and the admirable founder of Saint-Lazan, and of the Sisters of Charity, did not forget the little town of Brie, in the first attempts at religious establishments, which he planned at that time.

Faithful to these sacred and honourable memories, the virtuous duchess confided the new asylum to the intelligent and devoted care of Sisters of Charity. She added to it a little free school and a work room for poor orphans ; but it was not without great difficulty that she realized her holy plans.

It was in the very midst of this zealous work, that the good God afflicted her in the most sensible manner by calling to Himself her beloved daughter. This sad event made her resolve to reserve for herself the part of the church which for several years had been a pilgrimage of the Blessed Virgin ; to repair it, consecrate it to the cross, and to have a vault hollowed out to receive her Ernestine. She wished to have her near herself ; to pray over her tomb for the consummation of her happiness ; to find there the inspiration to do any good work, and from the hope of reunion to draw the courage needed to be faithful to all that grace demands.

While pursuing her plan, her heart is again saddened by a grievous loss. After being detained at Paris, to hasten the winding up of some business, she made great speed to rejoin her mother-in-law, whom she had left at Montmirail unwell. She set forth then, as fast as possible, with her husband. On the way an accident to the carriage having made the good duchess fear for a moment that her son was crushed to death, she experienced such a shock that her health was shaken by it for a long time. This was only the beginning of the troubles of this sad journey, As they approached home, the embarrassment of. the castle-servants, their hesitation in answering the eager questions of the duke and duchess, increased their anxiety. . . . . Their presentiments were only too well founded ; the viscountess had just expired in her easy-chair, without any suspicion on her part or on the part of those about her that she was near her end. The heart already wounded is more sensitive to fresh grief, and Madame de Doudeauville mourned with her husband a real mother, to whom the heavy trials borne together had knit her very closely. Amid her tears, there remained the great, the one consolation, of thinking that the sudden death had not been unexpected. From contact with her daughter-in-law, Madame de la Rochefoucauld had become as remarkable for piety as she had always been for natural goodness.

Now the project of making of Montléan a place of burial had raised many difficulties. Madame de Doudeauville encountered opposition where she least expected it ; but she followed up her undertaking with as much firmness as moderation, and finally triumphed over every obstacle.

On the 14th of September, 1804, the chapel of Montléan was solemnly opened. Monsieur l'Abbé Legris-Duval, in an eloquent discourse, announced the permission given by the sovereign pontiff to dedicate the altar to the Cross, and to celebrate there the two feasts of the Invention and Exaltation with full octave and rites.

Two days after, the remains of Madame de Rastignac were brought from Paris and deposited in the vaults at Montléan; they laid there, too, the body of the Viscountess of Rochefoucauld and the heart of the Marshal of Estrées.

Monsieur de Doudeauville was then travelling in Italy with his son and his son-in-law; the virtuous duchess, who ordered all the preparations for the ceremony, gives him the account in this simple and touching description : —

"MY DEAR FRIEND, — To-day the transportation of our beloved daughter is to take place. Pardon the details that I am going to give you, but I feel in my poor heart that they will interest you. I had not dared to mention the idea that possessed me, thinking it would be impossible ; but nevertheless I asked Arnolet, who from his attachment wished to be one of the witnesses, to assure himself of the condition in which she was. His manner of answering, after seeking information, showed me, that at the end of a year, it was probable that nothing would remain. But, to the astonishment of all, they found her as she was at the moment of her death, without the smallest sign of corruption, without odour. Arnolet recognized her perfectly. They uncovered her face only, but on changing her from one bier to another, it was proved that the whole body was equally well preserved. Why could n't I have seen her once more ! They said she had a beatific expression. If that, coupled with the heroic sentiments of her last moments, could give me the certainty of her present happiness, it seems to me I should be less unhappy. I shall have then in my possession, and you after me, and then our son, this precious deposit. May we all meet again in heaven !"

The new church, by its form, and the distribution of the daylight, recalled somewhat the image and solitude of the tomb. On the left of the little nave was a chapel dedicated to our Lady of Pity. In the middle of the sanctuary, raised five steps, was the altar, surrounded by funeral emblems, allowing one to see partially, beyond, a heap of rough stones covered with moss; and from this rustic mound uprose a cross formed of a pine trunk in the bark. This cross in the darkness caught the sombre light of a sepulchral lamp which the altar hid from view. Under the sanctuary was the vault destined for the burying. It was to the foot of this cross that the duchess often came to renew the sacrifice of all that she held dearest, and to fortify her soul by the contemplation of the sufferings and humiliations of the divine heart of Jesus.

The interest which she gave to sacred worship did not prevent her from directing, with admirable wisdom, her family affairs;

and her always increasing inclination for the mysteries of the Passion changed in no wise the charm of her intercourse and the sweetness of her relations with all. Good, devoted, vigilant, she takes in all her duties as wife, mother, lady of the manor, head of the house ; her eyes reach as far as her heart, and are never disturbed by passion. She has but one desire, — to do good, to relieve, to heal, to comfort, to preserve, to edify. This is the continual object of her thoughts, and mainspring of her actions. Grace has so penetrated her heart that she makes no distinction between express command and simple counsel ; the most perfect has become to her an imperious necessity.

With what tender solicitude does she watch over little Zénaïde, doubly dear by the ties of nature and as the sacred legacy of her dying daughter. She begins again with this child the task she had so well accomplished in the early years of her marriage, and fearing that the atmosphere of

mourning might sadden the years which
crave life and gayety, she gives her a companion in her games and her studies.
Thérèse Pérardel was just the same age
with Mademoiselle de Rastignac, and having been brought up with her, she never
left her, and became for the grandmother,
as well as for the little girl, a friend as
discreet as devoted, in whom they both
placed the most entire confidence.

It is a difficult thing to hold all the
powers of the soul in such perfect equilibrium that the discharge of one duty
should never interfere with the fulfilment
of another, and that a strong affection
should not sometimes become exclusive;
but this was not the case with the virtuous
duchess. Monsieur de Doudeauville has
kept carefully the letters which she addressed to him during the different jour-
neys which he took after the death of his
daughter. We see in this correspondence
the model wife who has perfect intelligence

of her duty; full of deference, she consults her husband on every occasion, and when she imparts her own ideas, she does it with so much tact and delicacy that she guides his decision while appearing only to ask his opinion.

"I hope you will not disapprove my little journey," she writes, "for in all that I do I seek to divine your wishes."

She is very attentive to the rules of the church, and knows admirably well how to couple the respect due to them with the considerations claimed by the health of her husband. She writes to him thus : —

"My dear Friend, — One thing at which I absolutely take exception is your resolution to fast while you are taking the waters. I request you to consult the doctor upon this point, and to do what he shall tell you. You have manifested your faith in a high degree by observing the laws of abstinence up to this day. I am convinced

that you would do yourself real harm in
continuing this longer. I do not know
whether my letter will reach you. But
what I know very well is that I am always
troubled about your health, and that the
consciousness of having been once mistaken is reassuring neither for the present
nor for the future, and justifies the anxiety
of every moment. I have a grudge against
my son, a little one against his wife, too ;
a great one against Raphaël, and finally
against everybody, except the doctor if he
has cured you."

In looking over these letters it is pleasant to find this good mingling of warmest
piety and tenderest sentiment.

"How happy you are to have been at
Annécy! I would give all the rest of your
journey for this one excursion, but not the
pleasure which I should have had in making it with you. How many moments of
rapture have I spent by the tomb of your

favourite saint! And how useful was his intercession in restoring peace to my soul, and in freeing it from the noxious vapours in which the sojourn at Genoa had enveloped it! What delicious expeditions among the poor those were! How many lessons I received! And what examples of virtue were given me! God permitted this, and the remembrance will always be dear to me! . . . . I feel moved in thinking of it, for my poor heart, torn with sorrow, does not keep back my soul from enjoying with transport all that connects it with its God; and this is the happiness of the Christian! Taste it, my dear friend; may all whom we love share it with us, and may we one day in heaven drink in long draughts from this fountain of delights."

As the courageous duchess had preserved the family property during the Revolution, at the peril of her life, Monsieur de Doudeauville was desirous that she should keep the administration of it. But if she accepts the trouble of managing the fortune, she wishes to leave the honour and the chief enjoyment of it to her husband, to whom she submits the details of any changes that are contemplated; of any measures that are to be taken. She awaits his de-cisions, she makes a point of what he or-ders, and if a discussion arises between them, they wish mutually to yield the right of settling the question.

This woman, so superior in all points, was endowed, as we have had occasion to see, with a great spirit of order and ad-ministration. She entered into the smallest details; revised the greater part of her ac-counts herself; made calculations; acted in concert with her farmers: it was impos-sible to deceive her. Her charity as well as her justice prompted her to this wise vigilance. She looked upon herself as the trustee of a property belonging to her children and to the poor. She who was so careful to avoid waste, and any needless expense, not only carried on her house on a footing suitable to her rank, but showed herself truly great whenever there was an opening for succouring or obliging others. She united two qualities as precious as they are rarely joined : perfect order and inexhaustible generosity. Extremely delicate in any question of interest, she was always disposed to give a judgment against herself when there was the slightest doubt ; she would then say to her men of business :

" I beg you, gentlemen, not to cause me to enter purgatory for a question of money."

The following letter reveals at the same time the just mind, the clear sight, of a woman who, undazzled by a brilliant fortune, wishes to limit her expenses to her income, and the delicacy of a heart which knows how to make an important sacrifice very gracefully.

" You will never find me severe, when there is a question of giving pleasure to others, and particularly to your friends ; you are quite free, besides, to use your fortune as you please, and you will never see me do otherwise than applaud or keep silence ; but I will tell you frankly that if we are rich, we are very embarrassed rich people. If we do not limit our charities and our expenses, we shall leave debts, or we shall encroach on our capital, which is the same thing, and which agrees neither with our principles nor with our affection for our children. All these reflections come to me from my present occupation with your affairs, and from the fright occasioned me by the incalculable number of our expenses, which are always on the increase. I doubt whether Monsieur de N—— will be able to pay back the fifteen thousand francs ; but I shall share the pleasure you will have in giving them."

In following the correspondence, we soon have the secret of these considerable payments ; besides the share of the poor, a

large set-off from the income, are numerous pensions for those who have rendered
services, and for certain persons fallen
from opulence into want. Madame de
Doudeauville had a particular regard for
this kind of misfortune. As for the sèr-
vants, they formed such an integral part
of the family that, once admitted into the
house, they stayed there until their last
breath. In their old age they were plied
with delicate attentions, and the best care
was lavished upon them in their sicknesses
or infirmities.

Where shall we find more faith, more
delicacy and charity, than in the following
lines, written by the pious duchess to her
husband : —

" MY DEAR FRIEND, — Your man from
Verneuil has arrived ; he is interesting,
and very glad to enter your service. But
you had n't told me that his wife is very
ill. I was confounded when I saw a poor

dropsical woman arrive, just on the point
of being tapped ; but I thanked Heaven,
and said to myself that it is by this sign
we should recognize that they are designed
for us."

Such generous sentiments should excite
gratitude and unfailing fidelity; in fact,
never were these so true and so oft repeated words better realized than at the
castle of Montmirail: " Good masters make
good servants."

One cannot read without emotion a page
in his memoirs when the Duke of Doudeauville, recalling the terrible invasion of
1814, comes back to what concerns his own
castle, and gives all the honour of its preservation to the courageous devotion of his
servants. But let us quote his own words :
" If our castle is still standing, whilst the
greater part of the neighbouring houses
have been pillaged and destroyed, it is to
the courage of our people that we owe it.

Being detained at Paris, we relied entirely upon them to take the proper care of defending our interests ; the principal responsibility fell upon an old family nurse who was in my house in the capacity of housekeeper. Her name was Langlois. For about two months she never went to bed, and in spite of her sixty years, she was obliged to meet the exigencies of the numerous daily visitors. Once, for instance, her energy was put to a severe test. Some Cossacks having been killed in crossing the country, their regiment came the next day to burn Montmirail ; by dint of supplication, a commutation of the penalty was obtained. Six hours of pillage in the town, two hours at the castle, were judged a sufficient expiation for the blood shed. The inhabitants on all hands had fled into the woods. Our housekeeper alone dared to stay at her post. Presenting herself bravely before the forty Cossacks who came to execute the order given out, she asked them what they wanted.

"'To plunder!' they answered, with a laconicism worthy of Sparta.

"'Very well; I will show you the way and open the doors for you,' she said, without losing her head. She did it, though, to prevent all disorder.

" In the two hours' duration of this performance, she remained among the men, restraining them as best she might, allowing nothing to be broken, and even preventing them from carrying off the most precious things. This admirable conduct and rare courage left their mark upon the memory of the strangers, and eight or ten years after, a prince royal of Prussia asked one of my relatives, at Saint Petersburg, if this good lady, who kept them all respectful, was still in existence. She could not save from destruction, however, our poor merino sheep. She had found some protectors whom she placed herself, like a general, so that they called her General Langlois. But the soldiers had invented a new kind of fishery which they found much to their taste. They had partly taken up the tiling of the lofts above the sheep yard, and through the holes made in the floor they let down ropes, with which they fished up the rams and the sheep, and were highly pleased with their succulent catch; we lost at this game nearly two hundred merinos, but the originality of the invention made us laugh.

"Once Napoleon dined at our castle; another time he slept there. This night came near costing us dearly. Finding his chamber too small for his big maps, he wished to have what he called the partition knocked away; but our good Langlois resisted him as she did everybody else, and the partition, which was nothing less than a wall three feet thick, was saved.

"Though the Cossacks fell upon all whom they met, and made them act as guides, sometimes causing them to perish through fatigue and beating, my poor steward, Gallet, in spite of his seventy years, explored our farms, his stick in his hand, and cast about him for ways to ward off or remedy the devastations.

"As to my valet de chambre, Raphaël, the faithful companion of my exile, he gave me new proofs of his devotion. In a letter which chanced to reach me, he informed me, 'They are fighting in the town, they are fighting in the courts of your castle; the balls reach the chamber where I am writing. I do not know what will be our fate; but be sure that to the last we shall show ourselves worthy of such good masters. I would only recommend to you my poor children.'

"We sent word to them in every way, to leave everything, to give up everything, assuring them that we would much rather lose all than to make them run such terrible risk, or even to leave them exposed to such trial. Not one of them yielded to our prayers; and even the servants whom we had at Paris begged us to let them go and aid their comrades to save our property. How much touched we were, and thrilled, by such proofs of attachment, and how they made amends for all our losses!"

In her practice, the virtuous duchess looked upon the little and great domestic vexations as a particular mark of favour, which, in calling for the exercise of charity, quietly increase the number of humble and solid virtues. Reproving the persons placed under her control with gentle firmness, she chose with good discernment the suitable time and way for giving directions; but she bore with unchanging patience the tempers, the natural imperfections, and even the faults of character which she considered incorrigible. She never complained of them, and her example as well as her advice won the others over to this mutual support, indispensable to the preservation of the union of hearts. Her presence of itself dissipated any cloud arisen

between two persons ; her expression of serenity made the peace of heaven pass into
all who approached her ; they felt that she
was continually in the presence of her
God. But her inexhaustible kindness did
not prevent her from being dignified and
imposing, especially if she had a lesson to
give. A civic priest, having introduced
himself into her house, in spite of the protest, found the duchess alone, seated in the
parlour ; she did not rise to receive him,
and she did not offer him a seat ; but he,
retorting by insolence, took one without
ceremony. She rose immediately, and listened, standing, grave and cold, to what he
had to say ; disconcerted by this attitude,
which was a more expressive reproach than
a long speech, the unhappy man made
haste to get away.

During the entire time of the intrusion,
she never appeared at any of the parish
offices, and had mass said in her oratory
by some faithful priest.

She took great heed never to scandalize any one, according to the counsel of the Apostle, who exhorts us to consider the weak. Whilst she was at work on the ornaments for the church, she would often occupy her spare hours on Sunday in examining the week's work, and in comparing it with the design, which she composed herself. One day, when she was thus sitting before her frame, surrounded by papers and pencils, she received a call from the wife of one of her farmers. Fearing that the sight of these instruments of work might scandalize the good woman, she tried to make her distinguish that this was not a servile work and contrary to God's law ; but she soon perceived that she was not and never would be understood, for each of her explanations received invariably the same answer: "Yes, madame, I see very well, each one works in his own way."

The pencils were forthwith laid aside,

and never reappeared except on fête days or Sundays.

It was not by accident, or circumstance, and still less through caprice, that the good duchess applied herself to handiwork; in all points like the virtuous woman, she understood plying her needle adroitly, and never lost an instant's time. The poor and the churches called out her zeal in this direction. The persons admitted to her intimacy found her always occupied, and her work was a great help to her in escaping from conversation when she saw fit. She was at times seen to be deep in her embroidery, and then all at once to come to the front, bringing back to the paths of charity those who were straying from it. As soon as she took up the thread of talk, they smiled pleasantly, seeing what she would make of it, for her reputation was thoroughly established.

This assiduity in work induced her husband to address to her the following verses,

which we shall quote to show the esteem
and veneration in which he held her:

> With virtues and charms well adorned,
> And all without any pretension,
>   My wife has still her head turned
> By this strange as it is a proud passion.
>
>   She delighteth to work without measure,
> This the object of all her desires;
>   While others run after pleasure,
> To work hard and well she aspires.
>
>   In the name of all the others
> On this *point* I a little must pause,
>   Full oft for the many are bothers,
> Of which thread and needle are cause.
>
>   For ourselves let us not go too fast,
> And at least say no word of blame,
>   Of merits the day is not past, —
> Good embroidery in *fine point* earns fame.
>
>   And therein is wisdom, in fact,
> For in all *points* what does not the man
>   Who gets and who uses with tact
> The very best *canvas* he can?

In winning approval from all
My wife in all *points* does succeed,
   Which a very hard work we would call,
Though to get it she takes but small heed.

Of her kinsfolk and eke of her sex,
Her talent, that brilliantly shines,
   Makes the ornament constant and complex,
Because taste with the rest she conjoins.

If everything please in her person,
It is so in her work and her mind;
   There is none wiser or better than this one,
For her first fault I never shall find.

In spite of my talent for satire,
Her *point* of my chief predilection,
   I must say, to be frank in this matter,
Is the very *fine point* of perfection.

As the Duke of Doudeauville was fond of poetry, and found nothing comparable with his wife, he took advantage of the slightest circumstance to express his sentiments to her in verse. Thus, on the teast of St. Augustine, he composed and distributed about him couplets adapted to

the occasion, where each found his compli-
ment ready for him. The good duchess
lent herself gracefully to these demonstra-
tions, which were not naturally quite to
her taste ; but one year these compositions
were multiplied to such an extent that from
morning till night she had the gratification
of hearing her praises sung by everybody
who encountered her. This day was so
painful that she conjured her husband not
to subject her to such a penance again ;
and he then decided that all his attentions
of this kind should come in future from
the mouths of the little children, who, as
she advanced in age, were multiplied about
her.

The real pleasure of this generous châtelaine was, on the fête days, to procure some
indulgence for the poor of the country.
This was her great delight ; she could only
be happy in the happiness of others, as we
shall see in the following passage : —

"I must tell you, my dear friend, that

being once established here, I should be very sorry to leave the place ; the same reasons which have attached me to it for many years exist and will exist until my last breath ; but they are all concentrated in a very narrow and very gloomy place. For the rest of the habitation, it has become for me what any place in the universe would be. I believe, that is to say, it is animated only by the more or less happiness which I see those I love enjoy, for my heart alone is not dead in me ; this is said only once in passing, and never to be alluded to. I do not wish to think aloud on the subject."

This dark and sombre place we know already ; unable to get there as often as her inclination prompts, the good duchess has in a secluded part of her garden a little hermitage, simple and solemn, where she loves to retire ; therefore, when, profiting by the permission she has generously given, the inhabitants of Montmirail come to walk under the magnificent shade trees of the park, they know that no one must force his way through a certain green belt; this is the retreat of the holy duchess. There, seated on the trunk of a tree, she has watched the ruins of Montléan rise again in the distance ; and while a dwelling for the God of the Eucharist and a place of repose for her beloved daughter were preparing, she has meditated long upon the instability of the things of earth. These reflections, while they incite in her the desire to reach the end of her exile, make her wish more ardently for the perfect accomplishment of the Divine Will.

But let us take care not to imagine that the inhabitants of the castle and their guests had anything to suffer on account of this charm of solitude which the holy duchess felt ; nobody did the honours of a friendly hospitality better than she ; one was sure to breathe a beneficent air in the lands of Montmirail in every respect. If one was always edified by the noble and virtuous attitude of the mistress of the house; if, after talking with her, one felt himself nearer to God, one had never to fear tedious exhortations ; a word, an impulse of the heart, revealed casually the ardour of her faith ; but she did not preach ; only, there was in her so great compassion for all suffering, that without any direct advance, one felt impelled to open his heart to her. Then, she was sure to drop a word which one could not forget ; he came back to her as to a vivifying spring. The young Viscountess de la Rochefoucauld, particularly, enjoyed and made the most of such good society. In 1806 Monsieur Sosthènes had married the only daughter of Duke Mathieu de Montmorency. "She was," says Monsieur de Doudeauville, "more adorned by her sweet piety than by the beauties of her person."

Married at sixteen years, of a timid character, she was happy to find in her mother-in-law a gentle and wise adviser; she hid nothing from her and told her her most private troubles with entire confidence. The good duchess loved and esteemed her much, and took pleasure in praising her. She had only to say to her, "My daughter, it is a duty!" All was ended, no more objection, repugnance ceased, and the young woman gave herself warmly to that which cost her most.

A close friendship linked the Dukes of Doudéauville and Montmorency, and when the latter, in 1811, was banished from Paris for having visited Madame de Staël, who had saved his life, it was in the Castle of Montmirail, with his friend, that he passed pleasantly his three years of exile. Madame de Montesquiou, in favour with Napoleon, had obtained this mitigation of his proscription. She was then governess to the King of Rome, "much against her will," says her brother-in-law. It was upon Madame de Doudeauville that the emperor

had first cast his eye to bring up his son,
but having sounded the ground prudently
first, he saw at once that he must not expose himself to a refusal, and he made
choice of Madame de Montesquiou. Let
us borrow from the memoirs of the Duke
of Doudeauville one sketch which proves
the firmness of character of this worthy
sister of our virtuous duchess : —

"The Countess of Montesquiou enjoyed
great credit and consideration from the
head of state. She made no use of it except to be helpful to others, and kind to
those who knew her.

"The way in which she came to this
place is curious enough, and deserves to
be related. They spoke of her for it, but
nothing was decided upon. She was at
Trianon, at a little distance from Bonaparte. He wished only seven or eight persons at his table. Not expecting to be
summoned, she had begged the chamber-
lain in waiting not to forget her two dishes

of fish, for it was a Friday; but all at once Napoleon had her told that she was to dine with him, and in fact, he put her at his side.

"More engrossed by her conscience than her honours, she saw with grief and embarrassment that there was nothing prepared without meat; but she began courageously to make her meal with butter. Her imposing neighbour looked at her and said never a word; but the confusion of my poor sister-in-law increased when she saw the dishes that she had requested appear on the imperial table. She thought that her host would take offence at such an impropriety; but she ate, all alone, the dishes they brought her, none the less. Napoleon still looked at her and said nothing.

"Everybody was convinced that this act would condemn her forever in his mind. Two days after she received her nomination as governess to the King of Rome. The Emperor of Austria, who was likewise one of the guests at this dinner, had not the same courage. He said, a few days after, to one of the children of Madame de Montesquiou, 'I admired your mother, but did not dare to imitate her, though I hold the same principles. She showed a character which filled me with shame and envy.'"

In all Napoleon's court, there was only Madame de Montesquiou who had the courage to speak frankly to him. One morning, when he came with Berthier to pay the young prince a visit, he said, taking his hand, —

"I hope it will know how to give a sword thrust some day!"

"And I hope," said the governess, "that it will have learned first how to scatter many blessings."

CHAPTER VIII.

NAZARETH.

WHEN Madame de Doudeauville saw the different works established at Montléan prosper in the hands of the Sisters of Charity, her indefatigable zeal projected the creation of still another : not far from the church, she had reserved to herself a modest habitation ; she brought together, there, a few nuns whom the Revolution had scattered, and she made for them a little boarding-school, composed for the greater part of children of good families, ruined by the misfortunes of the times.

Monsieur Legris-Duval was their first superior. He gave them in writing, not rules, for each one had her own, but very wise principles of conduct, designed to establish union and charity among them.

The new community took the name of the Ladies of Peace.

In spite of the diversity of minds which must exist among persons of totally different orders, the house acquired a good reputation abroad, and under the direction of the excellent Abbé Legris-Duval, the pupils imbibed principles of sound piety.

Like Madame de Maintenon formerly at Saint Cyr, so here the good duchess was the soul of the school, and she impressed upon the education the simple and solid seal of her strong and gentle virtue, inspiring the pupils with a spirit of order, of economy, of love of work, with the sentiment of duty. She desired to prepare them for serious women, useful and pleasant in the family circle, capable of sacrifice and of influence for good.

As long as the Abbé Legris-Duval lived, whose forbearance knew no bounds, the community seemed to be on good terms with one another; but after his death, each nun wishing to make her primitive rule the predominant one, the pleasant relations came to an end. At the urgent request of the good duchess, Monsieur Frayssinous, and after him Father Roger, tried in vain to pacify the Ladies of Peace.

These two men of large experience, struck with the wise and elevated views of Madame de Doudeauville, and despairing that they should ever see her attain her ends with such a diversity of minds, advised her not to permit the community to extend, but rather to let it die out gradually.

The superior, who had asked for authority to make a new building, and was displeased at being refused, secretly planned her departure, and passed over into a neighbouring diocese with her little colony.

This retreat, which was not to be regretted, caused the good duchess, notwithstanding, great embarrassment, — the ordinary signal for providential succour. She might have placed her young protégées in another establishment simply, and have given the house at Montléan up to some other purpose; but it seemed to her that the good God asked the continuation of this work. She had just married her granddaughter, Mademoiselle de Rastignac, to the Count of Rochefoucauld, and being thus left without a child about her, she was very fond of going to see her little scholars. Then, from this tomb where she sought her pious inspirations, she fancied she could hear a pressing invitation to perpetuate, as far as possible, her mission to the young.

This meditative soul, which learned a lesson from everything, and which passed from reflection to practice, always increasing its circle of well-doing and felt a need to associate itself with the movement of regeneration which was everywhere manifested. Knowing that one must build the edifice from the foundation, she was rejoiced at the enthusiasm with which some of the old and some of the new religious bodies gave themselves up to the work of the education of young girls ; but for this important task she had her own idea, her private thoughts, the fruit of experience.

If, as she had said to her daughter, that fallen grandeur, those ruined fortunes, that complete overthrow which she had witnessed, induced her to exclaim, " God only is stable ! " she drew from the uncertainty of the times and of things this other conclusion : the necessity of strengthening the character, of preparing a young girl early in life to endure reverses, not only in a spirit of faith, but also with intelligent and practical courage. She wished her to be initiated little by little, as far as her age allowed, into the details of domestic life, so that if some day the young girl should find herself obliged to serve herself, and to come to the aid of her people, she would not feel herself demeaned, and would not be strange to the work which Holy Scripture has so highly praised.

To attain this end, Madame de Doudeauville wished to offer, to the families whom modern luxury terrified, establishments more apart from the great world, where, in giving complete and distinguished instruction to their children, the special care should be to bring them up in antique and noble simplicity, to inspire them with serious tastes, to give them the habit of work, and in a word to fit them for good mothers of families and wise heads of houses.

To these principles of education the pious duchess joined a strict estimate of the religious life, which she wished to be perfect in its spirit, and very simple in exterior practice.

We remember with what ardour she sighed for the cloister in childhood and in youth. She wished to give herself up entirely. God, while accepting her offering, had kept her still in the world, and fixed her there against all her inclinations, but He did not leave sterile the first and holy desire of His generous servant. He predestined and prepared her a long time back to found a new community; whilst grace made to flourish in this elect soul the humble and lovely virtues of which the Holy Family has given us the example in the little hamlet of Nazareth, Providence allowed her to face all the difficulties of life, in order to offer to the young girls whose education filled her mind, an accomplished model of what they were to be for the family and for society.

Father Roger, who was endowed with a particular talent for discerning divine inspiration, thought to recognize it clearly when the holy duchess confided to him her plan of a foundation. Without foreseeing how she would be able to accomplish it, he advised her to preserve her little school.

Then she made a real sacrifice in separating herself for the time from Mademoiselle Thérèse, her reader and secretary, in order that she might take the direction of the few boarders left by the Ladies of Peace, until God manifested His will.

The little building was not to be made from the old stones; the vigorous chisel of Father Roger was to work on new stones. Let us say a word about this holy religious, sent by Providence to the venerable foundress to be the soul of the work which she was planning.

Father Roger, born at Coutances, in 1763, studied at Paris with application and piety, and received holy orders there. During the revolutionary storm he exiled himself in Germany, where some young ecclesiastics of his acquaintance made him enter the society of the Fathers of the Sacred Heart, which became later that of the Fathers of Faith.

When, towards 1800, his superiors sent

17

him back to France, Lyons opened a great field for his talents and zeal. He filled the little city with fervent associations, which, imbued with his zeal, continue to give themselves to works of mercy in the obscurity of humble and silent devotion.

In 1808 a new storm having driven the holy missionary back to his natal city, he raised from its ruins, and wisely governed the seminary of Coutances; but as soon as the Company of Jesus was reëstablished, in 1814, he abandoned his post, and hastened to Paris to solicit admission. After his first vows, he discharged the important function of Novice Master; then for twelve years, from 1818 to 1830, while established in Paris, he gave himself with all the ardour of his zeal to the exercise of the holy ministry, embracing in his immense charity all classes of society. Following the counsel of the apostle, he made himself all things to all men, if he might gain them for Jesus

Christ. The poor, especially they of the Faubourg Saint Marceau, were the particular objects of his favour. His compassionate heart could not approach distress without feeling the yearning to relieve it, and seeking the means to do it. "He was," says Father Guidée, "a man of lively and active faith, excellent in counsel; a consummate director in the road to God; always full of simplicity and directness; attracting, charming all who approached him, by his cheery and affable demeanour, and gaining all hearts by his obliging kindness."

Let us add to these outlines of exact truth, the witness of a priest who had known him well:—

"I don't know that I can tell you more than you already know concerning good Father Roger. I shall always recall with emotion his wise counsels, and shall ever bless divine Providence for having brought me into communication with him. . . . . .

During my retreats he said things to me that were really flashes of fire.

" I think I can see him now arrive in the evening at my house, after a fatiguing day; giving himself up readily to his natural gayety, he would say a kind word to warm the heart and put one at ease; then he would seat himself in his easy-chair, and when there, would talk to me of the good God with a faith, simplicity, and love which I have never found in any other. What faith it was ! .... If Saint Paul would know only the cross, Father Roger would know only his Credo. What simplicity ! .... To go straight to God by the shortest road, that was his maxim. What love for Jesus ! .... What clear intelligence of the mysteries ! .... How often have I seen him weep in speaking of that Jesus whom he loved so well ! .... How many times have I thrown myself at the foot of my crucifix after talking with him. Then, what a holy liberty he took in telling the great and the world's people, not the truth which flatters, but that which illumines! What tact in stealing into a heart in order to open it and gain it for Jesus Christ!

" With his naturally ardent and active character, the holy man could not have attained to this perfect affability, to this even and amiable kind-heartedness which all admired, without many efforts. One found him always ready to listen, to say the word which instructs, which comforts or reassures. Nothing can give an idea of the tone of his voice in speaking of the loving kindness of our Lord. I cannot forget the expressiveness with which he said to a person troubled by excessive fear at the approach of her communion : ' But, my good daughter, what has Jesus done, that you should fear Him so much ? '

" This compassion for those who suffer, this longing to come to their aid, made him beloved by all. Who could ever say how much this good father was loved and revered by the working class, by children, and the poor ? "

So soon as the pious duchess learned to know Father Roger, she put herself under his guidance; the savour of his words was pleasant to her soul — for those words which escaped from a heart burning with a love of God, were full of strength and unction. This kind of spirituality answered to the inclination she had always had for the hidden life; hence she consulted this wise director in all her works, and he, on his side, held his penitent in particular esteem.

By a providential coincidence, at about the same time when the Duchess of Doudeauville placed herself under the direction of Father Roger, she entered also into social relations and into association in good works with Mademoiselle Élisa Rollat, who was destined to be the first superior of Nazareth. These ladies became very closely attached. With a great difference of character, they had marked features of resemblance : an ardent and generous piety, the love of duty, the desire of perfection, zeal for good ; each sought the other with equal eagerness. But the perfect tact of Mademoiselle Élisa Rollat always recognized, even in the closest intimacy, the proper distinction of age and position. She had for the duchess a deference full of veneration. On the other hand the pious duchess, who silently admired her, showed her the fullest confidence ; she loved the frank gayety, under which a very serious mind was hidden. With Mademoiselle Élisa, she allowed her faith and piety to speak without constraint, sure of finding a complete conformity of sentiment. When these ladies left Paris for the country, a continuous correspondence supplied the place of their conversations. In this simple freedom of speech, Madame de Doudeauville lets the secret of her humble and strong virtue sometimes slip out. A few passages from her letters will help us to know her more fully.

"I leave on Thursday. Sad for thinking that I am going far from the resources which my weakness needs. But God is everywhere, and He lets Himself be found when one seeks Him purely and simply; ask for me that I may meet Him. May He alone be our study; may His Divine Will find no obstacle in our souls; or at least may His love triumph over them. These, dear Élisa, are the prayers that I make for you, and whose fulfilment I beg you to petition for me; that will be more difficult, but difficulties do not dishearten me.

"Adieu! I miss your visits and readings, much; you have inspired me with a real friendship, of that kind which life does not end."

Ten days after, she sends her news of herself. "Here I am in the most profound solitude. I find myself well thus, and too much to my taste. My character being independent, that which brings me into subjection at every moment must be more useful for me, and perhaps it may be only on account of my tendency to independence that I love solitude ; at least, I enjoy it when God sends it to me ; I would like to make a better use of it, but I believe I ought never to seek it, for it makes me too happy.

" The correspondence of Zénaïde is charming ; her children are delightful. Little Alfred pronounced the name of God yesterday for the first time.

" My health has been poor for a fortnight, so that I am positively stupid. God wills it, and I will it with Him. Let us love, dear Élisa, this Divine Will, for the accomplishment of which our good Master came on earth.

" Adieu. It is at the foot of the cross that I like to find myself with you. I have, however, the weakness to wish that you may not have crosses too painful to bear."

Father Roger was still another tie between these two souls; and hence, after a short stay which he made at Montmirail, the good duchess writes to her friend,—

"I think, dear Élisa, that I shall give you pleasure in sending you news of the person who interests you; his health is better since he reached here. People think he has much mind, eloquence, and elevation, and withal charming simplicity. My son loves him extravagantly. Monsieur de Doudeauville fancies him much, and my daughter-in-law appeals to him and wishes that he might be here whenever she is. He has had a great success, then, in our family circle, such as holiness and virtue will always have. He is so good, one finds there is so much to be gained from him! His lively faith has made a deep impression on me.

"You sent us some very nice hymns;

The Cross, Solitude, The Blessed Virgin, The Love of God, have been sung in the parlour several times, to the satisfaction of all. If you could compose one on faith, it would give great pleasure to my daughter-in-law, and to me also.

"Let us seek God, dear Élisa; let us seek Him purely. Let us love Him with all the capacity He has given us to love Him with. Let us love Him in His creatures, but let it be for Him. Let us seek the cross, humiliations. Let us give ourselves up to His good pleasure, and let us abide in peace. This is what I desire for you as for myself, and I see, without jealousy, that you will arrive at it before I shall.

"Since you want me to tell you about my health, I will say that it is not any too good, and I may be obliged to give up to it for two or three days. To do enough without doing too much, is a thing almost impossible for me to achieve, with my character.

" Adieu, dear Élisa ; I always forget myself when I am chatting with you. It is
one proof the more that I am not morti-
fied, that I seek my enjoyment ; but that is
allowed us, you know ; we must get benefit
from it, if in our pleasures we thank Him
who has united our hearts in His love."

When the Ladies of Peace went away,
the good duchess expresses her disappointment to Mademoiselle Élisa, but, as always,
her faith prevails over every other sentiment.

" Yesterday I received a letter from Madame de Saint Ambroise, who informs me,
after a six months' silence, that all her little
colony are going to M——. They are
going there to found a house, with the sav-
ings of seventeen years ; and mine stands
with its four walls, and the poor children
without a mistress. May God be praised !
. . . . Thank Him for this new cross, and
ask Him to make us to know His will.
There are painful things in connection with

all this,—many I feel very sensibly ; but since I have done nothing to bring about this unfortunate result, I look upon it as a permission of Heaven. I adore, and hold my peace." A little while after, her sadness changed to joy ; the pious duchess foresaw that her friend might some day become the foundation-stone of which she had need.

" Dear Élisa, your last letter, so good, so amiable and touching, gives me much to think about ; perhaps my imagination goes too fast and too far ; but, however that may be, it gives me hopes, which, if they are ever realized, will crown my wishes. I should be all the happier, because I have asked for nothing, and the will of God would then begin to manifest itself in favour of an enterprise which till now has seemed a foolishness."

The hope is confirmed ; the project of the foundation becomes a common work. Being too much occupied to write himself, Father Roger sends his counsel and suggestions through Mademoiselle Élisa to the holy founder. The commission is a delicate one, but the tact of the one and the virtue of the other smooth all difficulties.

"Once for all, don't be uneasy, dear Élisa; nothing that you say can trouble me. I know your motives too well; moreover, it is not my nature to attach too much importance to little things; and then, when I am sure of a person, he has the right to say anything to me. I desire in your correspondence confidence, frankness, and simplicity. You satisfy me in all these points, and amuse me besides by your gayety. Why, then, do you take such precautions about telling me that in Father Roger's opinion I am managing badly with Mademoiselle C——? The contrary would surprise me; but for me to be making a mistake is so natural! . . . . Never fear giving me pain on such an occasion as this." . . . . Always ready to find edification in, and to render justice to true devotion, Madame de Doudeauville, happy in seeing at the work a future member of the community of Nazareth, expresses her joy to Mademoiselle Élisa.

" I feel the need of telling you all my friendship for you, from time to time, and yield yet more to the necessity of speaking to you of our business matters.

" Mademoiselle Mouroux doubtless keeps you informed of the good order of the house, but what she is certain not to have spoken to you about, is the perfect way in which she acquits herself in her new position. She is overburdened, I am sure, for she has the care of everything, and yet does not look so very busy ; there is always the same serenity. I assure you that she is very virtuous ; the more one knows her, the more precious qualities one discovers in her, and the more heartily one thanks Heaven for having sent her to us. She is an angel whom God sustains, and who does the children great good. But be quite easy in your mind, she has no suspicion of my opinion of her; I intended this should be so, but, moreover, Father Roger also recommended it strongly."

These letters are dated 1820 to 1821. Whilst Providence prepares the way for Mademoiselle Rollat, and disposes everything for the foundation of Nazareth, the holy duchess is again fastened to the cross. For some time her sight had been sensibly failing; one day when she was reading her prayers in the chapel at Montléan, it had seemed to her as if a veil were passed before her eyes; the characters of the book getting confused, she shut it, made her sacrifice, accepted all its consequences, and appeared amid her family neither troubled nor afflicted by it. For two years she had to deny herself all reading, and could write only with great precaution. Having become totally blind in 1821, in spite of the urgency of her husband she did not wish the operation for cataract to take place; this was the way God had taken, she said, to withdraw her from the things of this world. What she did not say, but what she understood very well, was, that blindness, while keeping her constantly dependent, would also necessitate the perpetual sacrifice of her own will. What an exercise of patience for an active person, always accustomed to direct all the affairs of her house!

But in seeing her always serene, one would not suspect that it was a trial to her to ask, to wait for a guide ; she is so happy to do the will of the Master, and to have a shadow of likeness to Him! Were the divine eyes not veiled by the bandage on the day of the Passion? . . . . It is at this moment, when, more than ever, she needs her secretary and confidante, that she deprives herself of her services for the good of the little school at Montléan. Without laying any stress upon what must

18

have inconvenienced her, she is content to write to Mademoiselle Élisa : —

" I shall miss Thérèse on account of my blindness, but one must not count his sacrifices."

This little foundation has become the work of her heart. She occupies herself very much with it, while being entirely submissive to what God shall decide. Her purity of intention is always so perfect that, in spite of her desire to attach to herself capable persons, she writes : —

" Mademoiselle C—— has taken a great friendship for me ; we have passed eight days together. I have discovered sundry good qualities in her ; she might be very useful to us, and as she has grown fond of me, she seemed to regret her first refusal. I saw very well that she wished to bring about my saying, ' You would give me pleasure if you were to remain.' Not finding sufficient ground for bringing God's blessing upon it, I let her go.

"And here we are in great embarrassment. In the eyes of reason, we are doing many inconsistent things, but how good it is to put this aside sometimes, — this human reason! . . . . Monsieur Roger has assured me that it must needs be that people should ridicule us."

In 1822 Mademoiselle Élisa Rollat finding herself at liberty, the community at Montléan began to get into shape. It would be an error to consider the holy duchess as a simple temporal founder of this little society ; full of the spirit with which she desired to see it animated, she constantly practised the virtues which were to distinguish the nuns of Nazareth. If Father Roger, overpowered with work and charged with important labours, gives all his care, and devotes long hours to these few persons, joined together to imitate the laborious and hidden life of the Holy Family, it is that he has been struck by the living light diffused in a soul, whose holiness he admires so greatly as to exclaim : " I really do not know how God will manage to make her pass twenty-four hours in purgatory ! "

He is astonished, with reason, to find in a woman of the world such just ideas of the religious vocation, and these are not general notions ; she has her private thoughts, her project ; though the exterior plan is not designed, she sees clearly the end to be attained and the kind of perfection ; one would say that the Holy Spirit had been long preparing her for it, since in her meditations she has always felt herself drawn to contemplate the hidden life of Jesus of Nazareth. She had spoken of it so much with her children and grandchildren that Mademoiselle Zénäide, certain of pleasing her, had had the thoughtfulness to offer her as a specimen of her first work a picture of the Holy Family, copied after Caracci. In truth, another Divine Mystery had also great charm for the pious duchess ; she went alternately from Jesus the child of Nazareth, to Jesus on the Cross, and she would have liked to join in outward form what harmonized so well in her own soul ; but as it was to be a house for education, the name of Nazareth had the preference, — Nazareth at the foot of the Cross, having the Cross for the foundation, the cradle and support.

Finding, then, in the holy founder every sort of helpfulness, at Montléan they are not content with receiving her with all respect and gratitude, but they consult her on every point, and initiate her in all the details ; she is called upon to examine subjects, to pronounce upon difficult cases, and she treats each question with as much wisdom as humility.

She knows the religious and the pupils ; she watches the progress of her little protégées, takes much interest about their future, and tries to make one for them ; she is a mother and a saint for all the children of Nazareth.

On the holidays she comes, full of friendliness, to encourage their games, and to preside over their little literary meetings. Her gentle gravity is never a restraint, for nobody knows better, that childhood needs a full liberty of expression.

She had inspired her husband with the same feelings of interest and affection for the new community. Both of them agreeing that a house of education should not be placed next door to a hospital, and that the chapel should not be common to the pupils and the patients, they had made fresh sacrifices to transfer the sisters of charity to Montmirail, in order to leave to Nazareth the buildings and all the dependencies of the ancient priory. To this donation their zeal for religious worship had induced them to add a government annuity, for the support of the church.

The relations of the community with the Duke of Doudeauville were as simple as they were pleasant. He felt as much

interest in the prosperity of the establishment as his wife,[1] and seized every occasion to testify to Mademoiselle Rollat his
good will and devotion. He encouraged
the studies, distributed the prizes, and provided amusements for the pupils. Thus,
whenever the feast of Saint Augustine
came round, he did them the honours of
a grand lunch, with that perfect urbanity
which distinguished him until the end of his
days. His presence and protection never
caused the smallest embarrassment, for, in
his respect for the religious rule, he would
inquire the convenient time, would arrive
on the instant, and had for every occasion
the appropriate graciousness which doubles
the value of a service. The good duchess
was happy in seeing his interest in her

[1] The details of the community and the boarding-
school of Nazareth are naturally reserved for the life
of the Reverend Mother Rollat, the first superior of the
society, which will be a separate work, a sort of continuation and supplement of this.

community, and he, on his side, delighted to give his wife this sweet satisfaction.

It was especially in times of difficulty that the generous founder came to the aid of Nazareth. When, in 1830, Father Roger, obliged to take up the road of exile, trembles for the fate of this little religious family, which the Revolution has deprived of all its resources, the good duchess appears to him as his real Providence. He writes to her and renews his thanks more than his charges.   .

"MADAME LA DUCHESSE, — At Lyons I heard of the sad days of Paris ; all my anxiety is for you, and for my dear sister Rollat, of whom I eagerly desire tidings.

"Oh, how fortunate one is at this time to have a crucifix ; to know, as you have known for long, how to read the ineffable book and to find there a sovereign remedy for so great hardships, sorrows, and afflictions, which plunge the soul into an ocean of bitterness! Happy she who lives by faith, and who, peacefully occupied by domestic matters, leaves to God the care of directing for His glory the divers events which agitate governments. She lives in peace amid convulsions, and finds her repose in the accomplishment of the divine will. The Lord, always good and full of pity, will preserve under the wings of His Providence the poor little creature, who in her anxiety and alarm looks upon herself as lost, and yet wishes to have no other resource and asylum than the divine heart of Jesus. How well I love to see these amiable sentiments, which you share so fully with her, in my good sister, and how happy I should be if I might take part in your conversations! Be assured, madam, that I am in heart in the very midst of you all, and that I do not cease to present you both to the Lord."

When the terrible scourge of 1832 makes

its appearance, the good father reassures and strengthens them.

"I know your feeling, madam, enough to be persuaded that even amid epidemic disease you will lose neither your peace of soul nor repose of heart. You are too resigned to the will of God to wish anything different from that which He wills. Besides, He does not need the cholera to take from us a life which belongs to Him, and of which He is master. Let us live peacefully and without anxiety. Say this, please, to Mademoiselle Rollat; I do not wish that any one should be able to offer to one of my daughters the reproach which our Lord addressed to Saint Peter: 'O thou of little faith, wherefore dost thou doubt?'

"Give yourselves up to Him; and above all put no faith in the multitude of prophecies which agitate the mind, excite the imagination, and prevent each one from doing what God asks of him.

"May the Lord preserve you long, madam, for the happiness of your own family and of that which you have adopted ; may He give me the blessing to see you again, and to continue with you the excellent work which we have undertaken."

But alarm quickly fills the father's heart, and he who has reassured and comforted, has need to be consoled in his turn : —

" Since I wrote to you, Madame la Duchesse, I feel an always increasing anxiety, and want extremely to get news of you, of your excellent family, and of our dear house of Nazareth. I can truly say my soul is profoundly sad, and that my Allelujah cannot bring it the semblance of joy. To my troubles and sorrows of mind I join fear and anguish while thinking of your griefs, of the danger which you run in the midst of this plague which is ravaging Paris, and in calling to my memory so many who are dear to me, especially my sister at Nazareth and her children. We are really now beneath the Cross, and

we feel its heavy weight. Let us often repeat our Lord's prayer in the Garden of
Olives. But in charity soothe my sufferings in telling me about your own. I
would rather know than be ignorant of
them, and I hope that God will give me
grace to be resigned to His holy will."

After so much suffering, at last they
have the pleasure of meeting ; but the holy
founder is absent. Father Roger wishes
that she should have her share in the common rejoicing.

"MADAME LA DUCHESSE, — You have
already learned, through Mademoiselle Rollat, the kind reception I had on my arrival
at Montmirail, from all, even the inhabitants, but most particularly from the family at Nazareth, who, without distinction
of person or rank, religious and pupils,
rushed in a body to meet me in the court-
yard, and expressed their joy in such a
sweet way, so respectful and so reserved,

that I recognized the peace of the Spirit of God, and was affected and edified by it. What a comfort it is to a father to meet, after long absence, his dear children in the Lord! . . . . The next day was celebrated, as was right, by a solemn mass in honour of Saint Joseph, and by that joyful merriment which belongs to a great holiday. May all the good that you have done in this house come back to you, Madame la Duchesse, and to your excellent family!"

CHAPTER IX.

HOPES AND FAMILY GRIEFS.

WHILST the pious duchess scattered
abroad the charm and perfumes of virtue
in all her relations and acts of life, the
Duke of Doudeauville, since his return
from emigration, pursued, amid political
commotions, a career of devotion to his
country and to the cause of the unfortunate. By turns, and at times simultane-
ously, president of the Council General of
the Marne and director of the Committee
of Primary Instruction of the Seine, he
sits in the Chamber of Peers, and takes his
place amongst the managers of the deaf
and dumb institutions and the hospitals of
Paris ; he embraces in his sympathy every
kind of suffering, and flies to the succour
of the poor, the aged, and the orphan.

Being nominated Postmaster-general in 1821, afterwards Minister of State, and member of the Privy Council, he becomes in 1824 Minister of the King's Household. It was the position that suited his character best, and it got him opportunity of aiding thousands of sufferers. Amid his multifarious occupations, which all had to do with the welfare of the nation, he took upon himself the duty of presiding over the sessions where the poor petitioners were heard. Once, seeing him spent with fatigue and teased with fever, people advised him to forego this self-imposed task. "It is not indispensable that my health should be preserved," he answered, "but it is that the unfortunate should not be kept waiting."

His kindness of heart was never weakness, however, and if he were eager to oblige, it was never at the expense of a firm, just, and clear conscience. He greatly appreciated the care given to education, and felt all the weight of this heavy responsibility. Having the chief direction of the pages, he discovered, with great pain, that the innocence of the new-comers was in danger from some of the older pages. Immediately, without consideration for name or position, he sends away the culprits, and resists their supplications as well as the warnings that he will incur the royal displeasure. This is his account of his interview with Charles X. : —

"The king called for me the next day, and said to me, 'Duke of Doudeauville, what did you do yesterday?'

"'Sire, my duty.'

"'You were terribly severe.'

"'I was only just.'

"'You have lost five interesting children.'

"'I have only punished them as they deserved, and besides, I did it as gently as was possible.'

"'What severe punishment for a foolish joke!'

"'A joke! Sire, such a one as corrupts youth, poisons places of education, and makes parents wretched!'

"'You should at least have notified me.'

"'I had not the time, for there was not a moment to lose, and my responsibility, as well as the morals of the nice boys intrusted to me, was gravely implicated.'

"'If you had spoken to me, I should have said to the parents, Your children are behaving very badly, and I shall send them home if they do not conduct themselves better in a month's time.'

"'Ah! Your majesty will find me very presumptuous, but I congratulate myself a hundred times that I said nothing about it, for my good youths would have been undone, and the house, too.'

"'For all that, if such a thing had happened, you should have acquainted me with it before taking any action.'

"'Sire,' I answered, bowing, 'I should obey your majesty before anything else;

19

thus, when the house is on fire, I will come and ask your permission to put out the flames.'

" The king was good enough not to be displeased by my answer," adds the Duke of Doudeauville.

Before the fall of royalty, the minister had thought fit to resign. Though retired from public affairs, he was still the defender, the friend of the unfortunate ; and, whether at Paris or Montmirail, his little children and other works of benevolence divided his heart and time.

In connection with the Ladies of Peace, we have spoken of the death of the Abbé Legris-Duval. This family friend had gone to sleep in the Lord in 1819, deeply regretted, not only by the family of the castle, but by the inhabitants of Montmirail, his piety and kindly charity making him beloved by all who knew him..

On his death-bed, he had promised the holy duchess to plead the cause of her son and daughter-in-law with God, for that they were so saddened by having no child. Some months after his decease, she writes to Mademoiselle Rollat: —

"The viscountess gives us for the first time in thirteen years very sweet hopes ; one scarcely dares to believe in them, but I am full of confidence. I pray you to thank Heaven, and to ask for this child a living and active faith. It is the prayer that I make before all others, and God is too good not to hear me favourably."

The hopes were realized, and Heaven was generous, for the Viscountess of Rochefoucauld in a few years became the mother of six children, who formed a graceful crown about her.

To the great satisfaction of their venerable grandmother, their education was intrusted to Monsieur Bernier, a virtuous priest, capable of training the gentleman and the Christian. The two eldest, Messrs. Stanislas and Sosthènes, stated in their earliest youth, that this was what they intended to be one day.

Their best time, that of the fine season, was passed at Montmirail ; all was regulated to promote duty and pleasure, and the good grandmother looked forward to the moment which brought her little angels to her, as the sweetest in her day. Nothing could be more touching than to see them, on the signal for their recess, surround her arm-chair, and respectfully kiss her aged hand. The holy duchess would smile with that indescribable expression of maternal tenderness which she always retained.

"Well, my little children," she would say, "has Monsieur l'Abbé told you very pretty stories to-day?"

"Oh yes, grandmother, very pretty and very old too ; but they are perfectly true stories ; perhaps you don't know them, or maybe you learned them when you were little?"

"Perhaps I did ; tell them to me."

And then would come the always new story of Adam and Eve, and of Abraham, to which the grandmother would listen attentively, the more that the little narrator would put a great deal of warmth into his action and omit no detail.

Madame de Doudeauville took a particular interest in the education of the eldest little girl, whose vigorous and ardent nature gave no presage of her premature death. There was such an exuberance of life in her, that the governess, while recognizing her rich qualities, was often puzzled to provide for this activity, and this imperious demand for motion and novelty. The good duchess would then interfere, and it was curious to see her sweet, calm face close to the bubbling ardour which she tried to quiet, while giving it at the same time the necessary food. The convent games served as encouragements and rewards.

Next to Mademoiselle Elizabeth came little Marie, whom a sad event placed wholly under her grandmother's control. The mother of this delightful family died holily in 1834. At the news of danger, the good duchess hastened to Paris. When they announced to the sick woman that her mother was coming to see her, —

" What mother ? " she asked.

" Madame de Doudeauville."

" Oh, that one : that is the mother of my heart," she answered, and a gleam of joy passed over her face. This sweet presence seemed a safeguard to her on the threshold of eternity.

After receiving the last Sacraments, she wanted to bless all her children, and counted them. Noticing that one was missing, she asked for it ; the good grandmother then had the presence of mind to cross the hands of the dying woman on the head of one of the children already blessed, and thus spared her the grief of knowing that her little angel was no more. At the moment when she was asking for him on earth, he was preceding her and calling her to heaven, having yielded up his last breath a few hours before his mother, in his little bed, which she wished to keep next to her's.

Griefs were now multiplying for the holy duchess. In 1833, she lost her son-in-law, Monsieur de Rastignac, who had not married again ; in 1834, her daughter-in-law, and a grandson ; in 1835, her sister, the Countess of Montesquiou ; and a few days after, while still bathed in tears, she was called to shed more over Mademoiselle Elizabeth, who, in full health, was carried off by typhoid fever at the age of fifteen.

Each of these losses made a fresh wound in a heart which, wholly God's, was still the heart of the family. When a twig is broken from the branch, it leaves a sad incision there. Father Roger understands this, and the faithful friend sends words of true comfort to the afflicted saint.

"MADAME LA DUCHESSE, — I unite myself to you, before the Lord, with all the
affection of my heart, and share deeply
the sorrows which yours is feeling. But
your faith tells you that every cross is a gift
from God, and that, in a submissive and
resigned soul, it will necessarily produce
an abundance of ineffable graces, and of
blessings for this life and for eternity.
You know better than any one, madam,
what the Christian would become if he had
not this support, which St. John of the
Cross calls the 'strong staff,' that sustains
us. It is the Cross that has saved the world,
— it is that which preserves it in shap-
ing the elect souls. It is the daily bread
of the just, the most solid food of the real
disciple of Jesus Christ. The more bitter
and sensible it is, the more it is like that
which our Divine Master and Saviour bore
for love of us. The very sign of the cross
is a blessing, and by the strongest reason-
ing, the reality of the cross must be very

blessing. The more one is bound to it, the more should he deem himself happy. I pause, madam, for it does not belong to the words of man to heal the heart; it is the work of the Comforting Spirit which is in you."

The infirmities of age are now added to the suffering of the heart, and augment the merit of patience. Father Roger under-stands and admirably touches upon the privileges of this precious condition.

"I easily conceive, madam, that though in very good company, your soul should feel almost in a desert, without the power of opening or communicating itself. It has an inner language which is not that of the day, and which can only be exercised in perfect silence. Oh! how eloquent is this solitude, this forsaking of the creature, this language of the heart! What inexpressible things does it not say to the heart of Jesus!

"Do not let us complain of being weak

and of seeing our strength and activity fail; our body must decay, to tend towards the dust from whence it came, and whither it will return, whilst the spirit should labour diligently to raise itself more and more towards heaven, which is its true dwelling-place.

"Do not then think, madam, that you are growing old. Do as I do, who seem to be growing young: the more we approach the end, the more joy and vigour we should show. Our great distresses should not disturb us, for that is what belongs to us, — our real attribute; they are absorbed in the Divine Mercy, by the merits of Jesus Christ, our only resource and our only hope.

"We will say no more about our being joined together in prayer, for this has been a settled thing for a long time past.

"Do you know the other day I did not like to leave Paris without embracing the two dear children, Stanislas and Sosthènes.

I wish to add here a word for Mademoiselle
Marie, whose little letter I received with
much pleasure. Providence, who has given
into your hands the education of this dear
little girl, will also give you everything
which is necessary to develop her happy
disposition, and to confirm her in the love
of true virtue. May she always be very
merry."

This little girl, of whom the holy religious speaks here, and to whom he
addresses a word or two in nearly all
his letters, had been, since her mother's
death, entirely under the care of the good
duchess, who was engrossed in preserving
her innocence and developing her inclination to piety. Father Roger heard her
first confession, and whenever he could, he
did himself the pleasure of explaining her
catechism to her. The good results which
she got from this had such an influence
upon her whole conduct, that the kind
grandmother abridged her conversations

with the reverend Father, that he might give a bit more of his time to his little girl. In the chapel and among the poor the dear child found her chiefest pleasures ; and her greatest recreation was to do a charity. When she was entering her tenth year, her Grandmother de Montmorency, thinking to give pleasure, sent her as a birthday gift a magnificent cloak lined with ermine ; but when they opened the box at Montmirail, the child burst into tears. They were all astonished, and called her attention to the beauty of the garment ; but she said, still crying : " What good will it do me ? I have a plenty of cloaks for myself already, but I have nothing to cover the poor who are cold. Ah, if my grandmother had only sent me the money that this fur cost, I should have been able to do a great many charities."

Monsieur Georges de la Rochefoucauld, her great grandson, was growing up by the side of the venerable grandmother together

with Mademoiselle Marie. The two children were nearly of the same age, and had
the same pious and charitable tastes. They
were very fond of each other, understood
one another remarkably well, and in their
recess the question was, who could dress
the little chapels best. To please them, all
the inhabitants of the castle would go and
sing Christmas carols before the manger in
the parlour. They made pleasant company
for the good grandmother, who went over
her reminiscences to instruct without tir-
ing them. She had many stories to tell,
histories of the Revolution of thrilling interest, but in which she always put herself
in the background, in order to bring out
her relatives, friends, and servants, and
above all, the action of Providence. She recalled her fears, dangers, and privations:
as how one evening in the time of the
famine, being sad at having only one egg
to divide between her two children, she
had prayed, and had felt much comforted,

when, on breaking the egg to have it cooked, she had found in it two yolks, which, under the circumstances, made a real meal. They hung upon her words; she mingled with her narrative short but telling reflections, adapted to the capacity of her little audience, making them appreciate the usefulness of being able to wait upon one's self, of learning to be content with little, and the importance of being ready for every event.

The children would interrupt her by a hundred exclamations: " You saw all those dreadful things! . . . . You had no maid ! . . . . You suffered all that ? " . . . .

Who does not know the power of contrast over the young imagination; the privations of which their aged grandmother spoke seemed the more palpable, because, very naturally, the children compared them with the well-being that surrounded them. Then came their indignation against the authors of such great evils, those who had killed such good relations, — for in the Rochefoucauld family were counted thirteen victims of the Revolution. To this vehemence the charitable grandmother would answer in the words of our Lord on the cross: "They know not what they do;" and she would add, humbly: "My children, if the good God had not helped me, I should have done even as they." Whilst Mademoiselle Marie, grave and sweet, struggled to understand how she who was goodness personified could ever have been so wicked, Monsieur Georges, less serious than his cousin, would laugh roguishly, and taking advantage of his grandmother's blindness, would make signs to the others that he did n't believe a word of it; but from time to time, to cheer the conversation, when some new crime was spoken of, he would say: " You would have been capable of doing the same thing, would n't you, grandmother?" Delighted to hear her repeat her act of humility, he would multiply his incredulous protestations, and his gestures of reverent devotion.

The old manor-house, which had been honoured by the long sojourn of Saint Vincent de Paul, had now the privilege of sheltering a future apostle and martyr to the faith. Monsieur Olivaint, tutor to Monsieur Georges, was now beginning with modest gravity and intelligent devotion, his mission to youth.

That power of fascination which made the ministry of the fervent Jesuit so fruitful, was very happily felt during his stay in Montmirail : the soul of all good works, he organized there the Society of Saint Vincent de Paul. Such a character soon won the esteem and admiration of the pious duchess, while he experienced in her presence the respect that holiness induces. This holiness was to go on growing to the end, and to nourish itself at the fountain of sacrifice ; the death of Father Roger, which happened in 1839, while depriving

Madame de Doudeauville of an excellent friend and experienced guide, also took from her her powerful auxiliary in the foundation at Nazareth.

She had to make a great act of faith, that she might not tremble for the future of a little society hardly formed. The holy religious, a fortnight before his death, had written to her the following letter : —

" MADAME LA DUCHESSE, — I must indemnify myself for having been so long without writing to you, but it would be difficult for me to tell you all I should like at this moment. So many things come into the mind at the end of one year, and the beginning of another! As there is nothing stable in this lower world, and as the greater part of mankind, even Christians, find only those things fortunate that affect their temporal affairs favourably, I see very few who flatter themselves that the year has been in accordance with their wishes. For me, while seeing ground for alarm and fears, I do not give up the hope of having a truly good year, and I wish you the same. Your soul, madam, is too firmly established in the way of faith, and in the love of the divine will, for you not to find all things very good. What new happiness does the Holy Family prepare for us this year? It is a secret, but whatever it be, it will be great, for it will be in the ordering of Providence, and it will turn to the good of your dear Nazareth."

The good duchess needed to have learned to judge quite differently from the world, in order to bear the trials that succeeded; the charming child whose precocious holiness was her comfort, attacked by a lingering but incurable disease, after having given edification to her family and all the servants, passed away piously on the day of the feast of the Immaculate Conception.

A letter from Mother Rollat gives us some precious details of this death.

"Poor little Marie yielded to her long sickness on the 8th of December. She died as she had lived, with the piety and sweetness of an angel. Her happiness is not doubtful; even her present happiness is hardly so; but nevertheless pray and ask prayers for her, for we do not know the judgments of God. She received the Holy Viaticum twice, and Extreme Unction on the evening before her death, and all with perfect consciousness up to the last moment. She kissed with touching tenderness the true cross and the medal of the Blessed Virgin. A little before her death, they had placed near her bed a statue of that dear mother; she gazed at it with an ineffable smile; all at once, as if ravished in ecstasy she cried, holding out her arms to the holy image, 'Ah, how beautiful she is! How beautiful she is!' Then, moving her lips to pronounce the name of Mary, she breathed her last. They kept her for twenty-four hours, the face uncovered, and she remained as beautiful as an angel. After taking her to the parish church, they brought her to our own to be deposited in the family tomb. In spite of the weight of the leaden coffin, the congregation of religious would not give to others the consolation of carrying it. All the town followed ; there had to be guards at the door of our chapel, the court and even the main road being crowded. The family wished no ceremony ; the public grief and lament of the poor were more touching and beautiful than you can imagine.

" Madame la Duchesse is to be admired for the courage with which she bears a, to her, irreparable loss. This child was the delight of her life, and the object of her constant occupation. She stayed by her bed until the last breath, without shedding a tear, without the least sign of weakness ; then, having prayed, she went peacefully to mass and made her communion. It was only when her two little grandsons, Monsieur Stanislas and Monsieur Sosthènes threw themselves into her arms as she came back from service, that she could weep."

To crown all these trials, the Lord called to Himself, on the 2d of June, 1841, the honourable and virtuous Duke de Doudeauville. For two years he had suffered with heroic patience acute and almost constant pain, using the small intervals which his disease allowed him, to interest himself for the poor, and all that concerned the good of the country.

His uprightness, devotion, and pious resignation had impressed upon his face, worn with illness, a truly patriarchal stamp ; one felt himself before a man of virtue.

As, during the last months of his illness, he could not go to church, Monseigneur, the Bishop of Chalons had authorized the ordinary at Nazareth to celebrate the Holy Sacrifice every Sunday in the chamber of the noble old man. It was a favour which he appreciated, who in the midst of the greatest occupation, had made out a list of the benedictions given in the churches of Paris, in order to be able to receive every day in the week a benediction of the Holy Sacrament. He whom he had loved to visit came now to visit him, and entirely given up to the happiness of this Presence, he took no more interest in the affairs of this world. Thus, when the good duchess, to whom he had often expressed the desire of seeing his son marry for second wife Mademoiselle Vertillac, came to tell him the happy conclusion of this marriage plan, he stopped her by a sign, and said to her distinctly, "I wish to know nothing more of the things of earth."

It was with this sentiment of lively faith that he received the last sacraments. The entire population crowded to honour his funeral service, and do homage to a generous benefactor.

CHAPTER X.

WE approach the end of this long existence, where fidelity grew with trial, and love with fidelity. Before seeing it close, calm and serene, according to the promise of Holy Scripture, like the evening of a beautiful day, we wish to reproduce a portrait sketched by friendship, and preserved among the family relics.

"In the old Castle of Montmirail lives the octogenarian whom all approach with veneration. Age has not changed her regular, noble, imposing features; it has but added to the majesty of this fine face; it has only replaced the charms of youth by those of grace and virtue.

"Strangers admitted to the antique manor; all you who approach with emotion the lady of the mansion ; you who know the purity, the uprightness of this long life, so well filled by the accomplishment of every duty and the exercise of all the virtues, — you are ambitious of the honour of pressing your lips to that venerable hand which has only opened to give or bless ; this hand, on which children and grandchildren come to put their kisses, ... but your emotion is doubled when you see that this expression of respect and tenderness is the only sign now by which the old lady can recognize her son and grandsons. Sight is lacking to this lovely soul, for the expression of benevolence and kindness.

" If the fine eyes of the Duchess of Doudeauville have ceased to see the light, her mind is clear-sighted, and her intellectual faculties have kept their youth. Born with a very lively imagination, and a very ardent soul, her reason has always been so powerful, that she early learned to modify and restrain her flights of impulse.

"If her severity was ever great towards all that was not perfectly pure, elevated, worthy, and Christian, she had for the sinner whom she was trying to bring home, extreme indulgence, one might almost say, a particular charm.

"Her exterior is calm; but her words are full of warmth and enthusiasm when she addresses those she loves, or indeed the unhappy whom she would comfort.

"She had successes without having sought them; admirers without deigning to receive their homage; she has sometimes excited envy, but neither calumny nor slander has ever dared to attack her; for the excessive severity that she practised towards herself did not hinder her from judging others with charity. Who could have wished then to look for the weak side of so fine a character? . . . .

"It was in religion that all the force of her soul took refuge; it is to religion that she owed the lessons which enabled her to

walk with a firm step to the end of her
honourable life. . . . .

" The rudest trials, during the horrors of
the Revolution, put to the test her heroic
courage, whilst neither threat nor danger
could make her yield or draw back one
step. She compelled those who were about
to send her to the scaffold, to admire her.
The most cruel sufferings impaired her
health, without being capable of shaking
her resignation.

"The Duchess of Doudeauville has even
more loving kindness than sweetness, and
her heart is very tender, though her sensitiveness has nothing feminine. If she
has never sought to shine in the world,
to make up for it, she is the charm of her
intimate circle.

" Her mind is universally just, and her
judgments are always based on considerations of a superior order.

" She is fond of serious reading ; an elevated mind attracts her, a generous senti-

ment touches her, and misfortune elicits all her sympathy.

"That is the Duchess of Doudeauville, with certain contrasts of character, of mind and heart, in addition, which give the more piquancy to her personality.

"May this model woman, so worthy of admiration, be long spared to those who love and venerate her, for the edification and example of the world!"

Between these grand lines, so admirably drawn, let us read above everything else, the saint; let us not forget that faith and love of God have put into exercise all the faculties of a superior nature, which, without the compass of religion, might have wandered into vain theories, like so many others, and whose life might have run out in unfruitfulness, whilst dreaming of the most generous devotion. How many good works; how many souls saved through her medium! What constant edification there has been for all who came near her! One

might say that every step has been marked
by a good deed. Do not let us deceive
ourselves ; grace alone can effect such miracles, and to be such as she to the very
end, without ever contradicting one's self, a
pattern of duty and apostle of love, one
must know well how to draw strength from
the source of holiness and infinite goodness.
It was by prayer, by habitual prayer, that
this woman filled her soul with the treasures which she poured out about her ; this
was the secret of her power. Prayer, union
with God, the understanding of sacrifice,
this is what made her invincible. Thanks
be to God, the spiritual life knows no pause ;
the soul goes on always mounting, — detaching itself more and more from earthly
ties ; all conspires towards the great work,
whose merit grows in proportion as the
will has greater efforts to make, and finds
itself less seconded by nature.

Now that the duchess can do no more,
actively, her heart makes up for the lack of

everything. Condemned to physical pow-
erlessness, she likes to keep herself in continual dependence, not only upon the divine will, but also upon the creature.

How many times, when eager to hear
letters read which bring her very dear
news, has she repressed this natural impulse and waited patiently until her secretary came to offer her services.

She gets up very early, and, not to disturb the household, she walks, leaning on
the arm of an old servant, to hear mass
at Montléan, nearly every day. In spite of
the injunctions of her children and the
example they have set of most respectful
deference towards the holy old lady, the
persons attached to her particular service
have adopted towards her an exacting manner, which she apparently does not notice,
and even encourages by her promptness in
submitting to all their arrangements. It is
not through weakness that she does this ; .
she has never been familiar with them, and

has always preserved the most perfect dignity, but she makes herself subject, through
a spirit of humility and mortification.

This virtuous characteristic is especially
remarkable, when, at nine o'clock regularly,
old Marie comes to the drawing-room
to lead her to her bed-room. One of the
habitual visitors at the château, seeing the
promptness with which she always rose,
after this summons, took it into his head,
for several days, to turn the conversation
upon a particularly interesting subject, and
to make it very animated at the moment
when this good but brusque woman came
to call her mistress. He did not succeed
in detaining her : one only time, however,
he accomplished making her hesitate for a
moment or two. Marie had time to repeat,
" Madame la Duchesse, it is nine o'clock."
In getting up to follow her, the holy woman
addressed a word of excuse to her.

When she goes to the convent, as she
does not wish to trouble the regular silence

of the corridors, she has asked to be notified when she enters them, and this Marie
does rather roughly, hitting her on the
shoulder several times, without drawing
any sign of displeasure from the venerable
duchess. Far from complaining, she ex-
cuses all this bluntness, and speaks of the
people of the castle only to praise their
devotion and good qualities.

Her toilet, while always very simple, is
for all that worthy of her ; she would not
wish to sadden those about her by the
smallest omission of the conventionalities.
She has, however, a great desire to be eco-
nomical, so that she may be able to give
more to the needy. In one of her visits to
the convent, happening not to have with
her her ordinary adviser, she begs the superior to tell her plainly whether the garment she wears may be mended again.

A poor woman seriously ill, having died
one day from the consequences of a long
walk which she took in order to catch the

duchess' carriage, that she might bring her suffering to her notice, the respected old lady not only has the three orphans whom she leaves brought up, but, touched by the frightful accident, and not being able to see for herself, takes care to be informed every time she drives out, whether there are any poor persons in the neighborhood.

· Towards the end of 1841 this worthy mother of Nazareth and of the poor had a keen sorrow to bear, which again threw into relief her burning charity. For many years, having given over to her husband all her income, she had reserved to herself only an allowance for her dress and her maid. It was from this sum that she stole her charity money, wishing to leave no mark of it. Monsieur de Doudeauville attached his name to all the well known schemes of benevolence. "One must give an example," he would say, "when one has a title and a fortune."

The pious duchess saw him pursue this

course with pleasure, in accordance with the advice of the Apostle: " Let your light shine before men ; " but so far as she herself was concerned, she clung to practising the words of the Divine Master : " Let not thy left hand know what thy right hand doeth." She liked particularly to help those poor people who are ashamed to beg. When her husband rallied her upon the subject, she contented herself with smiling, and casting a look at the Holy Family.

As she had seen, during the years which followed the Revolution of 1830, the temporal embarrassment of the house of Nazareth (which would not have been able to support itself, but that Monsieur de Doudeauville came several times to its aid), like a provident and wise woman, she wished to secure the means of existence to this community, without encroaching in any way upon the family property ; for this end she economized privately, and put into the hands of her agent what she called her reserve fund, which would end by being quite an important sum. The good founder had full confidence in this arrangement, when one day her confidential adviser arrives at Montmirail, asking for a private interview. She begs Mademoiselle Thérèse to go for a walk in the park ; then Monsieur L——, finding himself alone with her, throws himself at her feet, and says, sobbing : —

"Madame la Duchesse, before going to La Trappe, where my confessor has ordered me to end my days, I come to beg you to free me from the obligation of restitution, on account of the impossibility of my repairing the wrong I have done." "What?" asks the holy duchess, "you have done me a wrong? . . . . Is it only towards me?" "Yes, madam, and since that time I am deprived of the Sacraments, and shall be so unless your generosity forgive me all my debt." "Rise, sir, rise quickly," she answers, with emotion, "I give you what you have taken from me." "But, Madame la Duchesse, a considerable sum is in question ; it is that which you ordered me to hold in reserve. I have played at the Bourse, and have lost all!"

The unhappy man had just gone out, and his words were still sounding in the troubled mind of the venerable dowager, when Mademoiselle Thérèse returned. The face of the holy woman was disturbed, — the redness of her face, the altered sound of her voice, all revealed an internal agitation which she in vain sought to conceal. To the reiterated questions of her confidante, she at last answers by communicating to her the scene which had just taken place. Then, stopping suddenly, "Thérèse," she said, "I have been wanting in delicacy : I assured Monsieur L—— that I would remit his debt, that I pardoned him, and I ought not to have made his fault known. Promise me never to speak of it to anyone whatever." She had to agree to this to calm the alarmed conscience of the pious duchess, who, in spite of her assurances, repeated several times : " My God, I have not been able to imitate Thee ; to reveal the fault which one pardons is not to pardon graciously."

This opening of her heart to her companion comforted her for all that, and as soon as she was convinced that the secret would be kept inviolate, she took measures to protect the honour of her agent. Having summoned him again, she had him tear up everything in his accounts which had any bearing upon the lost sum. She confided to him the design she had of endowing Nazareth, the great distress she felt at its being impossible for her to do it after this, and for all reparation she requested him to tell Mademoiselle Rollat himself all that had taken place. " It is Nazareth you have wronged, sir ; it is to Nazareth that in the future you should give whatever you and your mother can dispense with."

And, regarding this error as a momentary surprise, a passing temptation, she left to him the care of her moneys, and even doubled his salary, on the plea of his having a greater responsibility since the death of Monsieur de Doudeauville.

The stipulated confession was certainly made to Mademoiselle Rollat, who was seriously ill at the time, for Monsieur L—— having asked, in the name of the founder, to see her privately, she sent away her hospital nurse, in order to talk freely with him. But after the visit nothing betrayed the trouble which the first superior of Nazareth must have felt ; nobody in the house heard from her mouth a word which related to this grave confidence ; and the secret, faithfully kept by the three confidants, would have been buried with them in the tomb, if the unhappy agent, again being guilty, had not himself made confession of his fault, and of the generous pardon he had obtained.

In seeing the resignation of Mademoiselle Rollat and her unshaken trust, the holy founder must have comforted herself more easily, and been willing, with her, to commit entirely to the care of Providence the temporal future of Nazareth, which she had so greatly desired to secure.

The Lord soon asked a new sacrifice of her ; she learned that the illness of Mademoiselle Rollat was incurable, and in the middle of April, 1842, she made haste to return to Montmirail, to hold yet a little communion with her. This holy friendship, begun under pious relations, had grown with the fellowship of labour and sufferings ; trials, sacrifices, and contemplations of the supernatural linked these two souls closely ; thus the venerable duchess was sadly afflicted by the great separation ; but, attached to the work of Nazareth for itself, she continued to give it tokens of her maternal care as touching as they had ever been, and one can say that until her last moment she had a tender solicitude for the little society.

But now her strength failed rapidly. Her hearing became less keen ; she walked with difficulty ; exterior life receded from her little by little, but her soul's life grew apace.

She had a presentiment that the activity of her intelligence was about to desert her ; she prepared herself for this new suffering, and said one day : " I have made my sacrifice ; all that the good God shall will."

A little after, she fell ill ; an attack somewhat like apoplexy reduced her to a sort of physical prostration. Seated in her easy chair, almost motionless, one would have supposed she had no thought for anything, if she had not fully revived to answer when they spoke to her of God, of her children, or of Nazareth ; then she would smile, or make an exclamation which disclosed the vitality of her intelligence and her heart.

Father Varin came frequently to confess

her, and give her the Holy Communion. One day, as he was about to go, having discharged his office, the Duchess of Roche-'foucauld, stopping him, gave him a book on those of the Tyrol who had received the Stigmata : " My father," said she, " what do you think of these stories ; are they not very miraculous ? " For an answer the holy religious, raising his eyes to heaven, cried, " Ah ! madam, for me the marvel of marvels is to see this woman of eighty years, whose career has been crossed by every trial, ready to appear before God, and to present to Him her baptismal innocence."

There came a time when the two holy old people had not the strength to, raise their voices and make each other understand ; then Father Lefebvre had to take the place of Father Varin. As the holy duchess expressed no regret at this change, those about her thought that she had hardly perceived it, and had not remarked the greater interval which they had seen fit to observe between her Communions, now reduced to one a week. But when, on a journey, the superior of Nazareth, stopping at Paris, told her that she had met Father Varin, and that he would soon come to visit her, they were astonished to see the pious invalid join her hands, and with tears in her eyes, answer, with great emotion: "Oh, perhaps he will give me back the frequency of my Communions!" Full of regret at not having surmised the suffering of such a privation, they begged Father Lefebvre to give oftener to the saintly dowager the God of her heart, her life, and her consolation.

A few days before her death she seemed to rally, her strength revived; they hoped to keep her among them for a little longer; but she, feeling her end approach, asked for the last sacraments herself, and as a preparation, desired that they should repeat aloud the evening prayers; noticing that they omitted the one she daily said for the

holy father, she asked for it. Father Pon-
levoy, who was present at the ceremony of
Extreme Unction, himself said the prayer
for the dying. The expiring woman gave,
to the last, sensible signs of fervour.

Her children surrounded her. They
hoped to get a word from her, an expression of tenderness. The Duchess of
Rochefoucauld, leaning towards her, said
affectionately : "Mother, do you still love
Zénaïde very much ?" No answer ; the
dying woman seemed no longer to hear.
Having several times repeated the same
question, and always without success, she
had the inspiration to ask : "Do you love
the good God ?" A "Yes !" spoken with
strength, made it understood by all that
from henceforward she wished to be occupied only by thoughts of heaven.

On the 24th of January, 1849, she died
quietly at Paris, at eleven o'clock at night,
in her eighty-fifth year. Her soul, detaching itself without effort from its earthly

prison, to fly to the bosom of the God whom it had so much loved, left to the material shell its majestic impress. One felt a religious respect in the presence of the temple where the Spirit of the Lord had so long rested. Children and grand-children, friends and servants, wept at the departure of the saint, the treasure of all ; but each, amid his tears, said those words of the church : "Blessed are they who die in the Lord !"

The venerated remains, being immedi-ately transported to Montmirail, were de-posited in the vault at Montléan, near those whose guardian she had been here below At the approach of the funeral procession, from all the environs the people poured spontaneously towards Montmirail, — or-phans, old men, entire families, who had felt the succour of the holy duchess, swelled a glorious cortège. Monseigneur de Prilly, Bishop of Chalons, associated his personal sorrow with the public mourning. The

332 Madame de la Rochefoucauld.

letter which he addresses on the occasion
to the chaplain of Nazareth is a short and
beautiful funeral oration, which we wish to
reproduce here to close this admirable life.

"My dear friend, I come to you, for I
feel that you have great need of consolation at Montléan, after having lost the venerable and generous founder who was the
glory and the chief ornament of the place.
If she did not pray for us in heaven, if
she had not left us her revered memory,
the treasure of her example, this loss
would truly be irremediable and irreparable. There would remain for us only bitterness and profound desolation, and we
should be excusable if we gave ourselves up
to discouragement; but let us take heart.
Madame la Duchess de Doudeauville is
still in our midst; she lives here, she will
live here always, her memory will be eternal. Ah, if we are not all saints, nothing
will have been wanting on God's part, and
we shall be without excuse, having had for

so long such a beautiful example before our eyes. They say, and I easily believe it, that when Monseigneur d'Hermopolis would speak of Madame la Duchesse, it was only in exclamations of admiration and veneration ; he could not express the sentiments with which so excellent and holy a person inspired him, — a person superior to all those whose virtues we now esteem, and whom we see, notwithstanding, giving great examples to the world. This illustrious and admirable woman raised herself so much above them that she seemed, one can almost say, of another nature than the children of men. As much by the power of grace as by her fidelity in corresponding to it, she was quite by herself in the fulness of all virtue ; in piety, gentleness, friendliness ; in amiable and lovely humility ; in a word, in all the qualities which transform into angels the poor children of Adam, to make them in advance inhabitants of heaven.

"It is a great and inestimable favour when it pleases God to give such examples on the earth. We should profit by them as much as we can, and not stay behind when we see to what degree we can raise ourselves, and advance in the road of virtue by constant efforts and daily labour.

"They will pray much at Nazareth and elsewhere for Madame la Duchesse, and they will do well, for it is a duty, but we must invoke her prayers. I should not be surprised if miracles were done at her tomb. As for me, I shall often think of her in my perplexities. She was a person of great judgment, and a lady of good counsel. Louis XVIII. set a high value upon her advice, and consulted her often. I shall do the same, and shall be the better for it; she will always be living for me.

"The details which have been given me of the funeral ceremony were very touching; the memory of them will be preserved. We shall recall the affecting farewells made to this admirable woman by the parish of Montmirail, as they wet with their tears the coffin which is to encamp among you until the resurrection day. It is a real relic that you possess ; may she cover you with her protection ! I ask it of the holy duchess for you all. Let us make ourselves worthy of her kindness in taking her for our model.

" May the Lord deign to bless Montléan, this house, the work of her hands, which was so dear to her. May this precious establishment prosper, and be ever an asylum, a school of holiness and virtue ! . . . .

" The heart of the daughters of Nazareth has rest and joy in the remembrance of her whom Providence inspired to create their little society.

" Happy in finding in her memory a model and encouragement, we make but one prayer over the tomb where admiration is mingled with gratitude : ' That pursuing from the heights of heaven her noble mission, she, whom zeal constrained here below, may now intercede to multiply the number of Christians who walk through life by means of the radiant beams of the faith, and that she may obtain the grace of fidelity for the humble religious family which she has so holily and generously loved!" . . . .

THE END.